GERALD TRITES

ISBN: 0986561509
ISBN-13: 9780986561504

BlackAvon Books,
Mahone Bay, NS

TABLE OF CONTENTS

THE SHIP TOSSED UPON THE SEA

It was at noon, when the monthly boat loaded with sugar cane arrived from Barbados and docked at the large government wharf, that Conchita Santa Maria Bolivar Conquez first saw Charlie Buchanan. He was walking down the wide gangplank used for unloading cargo and the first thing she noticed about him was the way he outsized all the dock workers scrambling around him. Then she stopped in the street and watched the easy way he walked among the other men and the way they didn't bump him as they did so many others. She also noticed that he was carrying strange things, including a very large thin black leather case, about three feet square, with a thick leather handle on one edge and a shoulder strap. Propped over his shoulder were some long sticks fastened together with leather straps and steadied with his left hand. In his other hand were two large black cases with shiny metallic corners. All of this he carried with ease through the milling crowds on the wharf and across the main street of San Cristobel to the big weather-beaten hotel facing the ocean.

As he passed in front of her at a distance of about a half block, she saw his sandy hair curling slightly in the soft breeze and could sense his raw strength as she watched his wide shoulders moving with the rhythm of his thick leather sandals. His loose, white cotton shirt draped down to the pocket tops of his faded blue jeans. He had, in her eyes, a mature look about him, but most observers would have guessed that he was still in his twenties, or maybe only slightly beyond. He had the easy, disinterested air of an experienced wanderer. She stood still and watched until he disappeared through the swinging doors of the main entrance to the hotel.

After he was out of sight, she resumed her walk across the street and then along the white, sandy beach beneath the long coconut trees that leaned out of the groves towards the sun and the ocean. She walked until she came to a small faded shack built on short stilts over the sand at the edge of the coconut grove. A few sandflies buzzed in and out of the square holes that served as windows, over which she had nailed squares of wire mesh to keep out the young boys who wandered the beaches at night and sold ganja to the few tourists who strayed from their compounds at the other end of the beach or else robbed them and then spent the money on rum sold through the back door of the old hotel by the bartenders. At other times, when the boys were bored and had no money, they would come around her little shack and throw coconuts and bread fruit at the weather-beaten walls and laugh that they were going to come inside and get her. But she would run out with her long machete and they knew not to come too close to her and would soon leave, laughing at each other and looking back over their shoulders as they walked together down the beach.

They knew that Conchita Conquez was not the kind to push too far. Her story had flashed through the town when she arrived from the barrios of Bogota a few years before with some ruffians running drugs up into the southern cays of the Bahamas. She had seized the opportunity they gave to escape the slums but their demands on her were harsh and one dark night off the coast of San Cristobel, she had rammed an iron spike into the side of a rough seaman's head and jumped overboard and escaped into the coconut groves. Next morning, the sailors docked and told their story and searched for her, but she hid until they left. The townspeople said nothing because they considered that she had done them all a favor. Afterwards, she lived quietly in the small abandoned shack by the sea and in the evenings was visited by sailors and other travelers sent to her by the dockworkers or by the bartenders at the hotel. In this way, she was able to buy the small quantities of food and other things she needed and also save some American dollars stuffed into coconut shells lying in the corner of the hut under a loose board.

Sometimes at night when she was alone, she would take the money out of the coconut shells and pile it all together in the middle of her cot and count it. She counted slowly in Spanish, the way she had learned from the teacher with long blonde hair who had stayed in her barrio one year. Slowly the amount grew and she dreamed of the shop she would have for selling nice things to the tourists, a shop like those she had seen near the big hotels at the other end of the beach. She would see herself wearing a pretty long pink dress and showing the women nice perfumes and gold bracelets and working the big cash machine by the door and smiling thank you to them as they left with their packages. Sometimes she would squirt some of the fragrant perfume on her throat and don a gold bracelet and sit in one of the big lobby chairs looking towards the main door and watch the young men coming and going. And sometimes one of them would smile at her and tell her with his eyes that she was very pretty.

By the next morning, Conchita had forgotten about Charlie Buchanan when she heard feet moving through the sand not far from her hut, just after the red sun had appeared above the gently heaving ocean. When she peeked outside through a crack in the door, she could see him unfolding the sticks he had carried the previous day and standing them up in the sand so they leaned against each other. He twisted a bar sideways near the middle and then pulled a square white board from the big flat leather case and set it upright to rest on the bar. Then he sat down on a box and began to place little colored jars on a shelf that unfolded below the bar.

He was facing the sun, which was hovering low over a spit of land jutting into the sea. He quickly began to sketch the outlines of the land and the sun and the waves dancing with points of light. He also sketched a big square-rigged ship tilting in the breeze around the end of the point. Conchita squinted hard into the sun, but could see no such ship on the water. She sat on the floor behind her door and peered between weather-beaten planks. She watched him without moving until the sun was high in the sky and he packed up his gear and walked off down the beach towards the town. By then he had his shirt off and her eyes followed his brown muscular back until it disappeared from sight.

Conchita watched Charlie every morning for a week and slowly saw the scene on the canvas take on a lifelike quality, but one much more turbulent than the reality, as though he did not see or did not want to see the calmness before him. The ocean seemed to roll and heave and the green trees on the point arched out and trembled over the water against a background of grey threatening skies. She realized that the square rigger was leaning into a turn that would take it out to sea, rather than into the safety and calm of the bay.

She had been at sea enough that she could almost feel the heavy wooden decks tilting sideways and jarring and sliding against the wind-whipped waves. And she had felt the fury of the sea storms, especially during hurricane season. Usually, the hurricanes started with heavy rain and high wind and built their terrible force on the deep ocean. Sometimes they moved towards the northwest and struck the east coast of the United States. At other times, they would veer eastwards out to sea and gradually lose themselves in the vast Atlantic. But some of the worst storms traveled westwards to the jungles of Central America and the white-gold coastlines of Mexico. Conchita had known the terror of these storms, had felt their screeching winds and awesome power.

One morning as Charlie painstakingly sketched the detail of the shrouds running up from the railings to the tops of the masts, she quietly opened the door, crept across the beach and sat on the sand a few feet behind him. He did not appear to notice she was there, but after some time, she became restless from sitting so still and shuffled her feet in the sand.

He turned and smiled. "I wondered when you were going to come out."

"Como dico usted?"

He said it again in Spanish.

"You were watching me."

"No, you were watching me," he laughed. She laughed with him.

She pointed to the painting. "It is very beautiful. Will you make a picture of me?"

He had heard about her from the men in the hotel. The bartenders had suggested he go to visit her, but he had laughed at them, saying he had never had to pay before and wasn't about to start now. But as he looked at her sitting in the sand with her legs folded under her, he could see why the men wanted her. There was a touch of hardness around her eyes, but also a kind of sadness that spoke to him of tragedy and survival. Her body still had the firm smoothness of youth and her hair flowed black and thick and shiny to her shoulders. Overall, she was incredibly beautiful, sitting there in the bright light of the late morning sun in her tattered and soiled red dress.

"OK," he said. "We'll start tomorrow."

The next morning, he arrived at the usual time and she was waiting for him at her front door. She had stacked branches and palm fronds against the trees in front of her hut to form a small sheltered area. She had also dragged a small bamboo settee outside and placed it in front of the door. She sat on the settee and watched him as he unpacked his gear and set up the easel with a new blank canvas.

When he finally stood to the side of the easel and surveyed her with a brush in his hand, she jumped to her feet. "Oh, you are ready," she said. Then she slipped her dress off her shoulders and let if fall to the floor and stood there before him. "How would you like me to be?" she asked. "Should I sit down or should I lay sideways on the chair or should I just stand here?"

He cleared his throat and tore his gaze from her firm brown nipples and black pubic hair and said, "Try reclining on the settee sideways." When she sat down, he moved her left arm so her head would rest on it and placed her hair to flow down over her shoulder to her breast. Then he asked her to look out to sea and imagine the old square rigger ship coming around the point so her eyes would take on that lonely, far-away gaze he had seen the previous day.

As he sketched out the preliminary lines, he was able to focus on the curves of her body and he placed her right arm along the rise of her hip, so the flow of the picture moved from her shoulders down along the slope of her legs to her feet. After a few days, he brought her a little bottle of red nail polish and after setting up the canvas, he painted the nails of her hands and her toenails and got her to wave them in the air to make them dry more quickly. While she laughed and waved her fingers at him in an extravagantly dainty manner, he sketched out the hut behind her and drew a small red light above the door, although at the same time thinking perhaps it was unrealistic for a small hut on the beach to have such a light.

Each day, he arrived at about the same time and they worked together until the sun was high in the sky. She was very patient and able to stay in the same position for long periods of time. While she was still, he was able to concentrate on the painting but when she moved a little, he sometimes lost his concentration and often he would pass her the dress and they would go for a stroll on the beach until the stiffness left their bodies, for he also moved very little while he was painting.

It was not long before he found he had taken on a difficult task. He seemed to see her differently each day. Some days, she would squint fiercely into the bright sky and would seem rough and wild. Other days, she would turn a tender look towards him, and he would see a gentle and vulnerable side to her. He saw the softness of her hair falling over her breast and the way her shoulders flowed smooth and round to her neck. And as the days went by, he stayed longer.

Each day while she leaned with her head on her arm, she watched him painting out of the corner of her eye while she was supposed to be looking out to sea. She saw the way his shoulder muscles rippled as he lifted the brush and as the days passed she saw that the look in his eyes was beginning to change. Then, late one afternoon as the sun was low in the sky and his shirt was hanging on the side of the easel, he was painting with long slow strokes when suddenly she arose and walked towards him. He sat motionless, because she had not picked up her dress, and she took him by the hand and led him into the hut to her cot and pulled him down on top of her.

When he entered her they moved together as one and she floated like a white cloud drifting beneath the sun on a lazy warm day. He moved in her with his whole body and mind lost in their slow movement together and in the warmth of her arms and legs around him. They drifted together long after the peak of their loving until slowly he noticed that his weight had borne down on her and she was breathing in short gasps. He rolled over and out of her and then gathered her to his chest and they fell asleep, tangled together, until the first rays of the moon entered through the cracks in the walls and then they made love again.

After that night, he would paint her in the mornings, and in the afternoons they would stroll around the point of land jutting into the ocean to a small secluded lagoon and go swimming in the warm salt water or lay on the beach together or make love in the shadows of the coconut trees. They would return to her little home when the sun went down and cook fish over a small charcoal fire on the beach. Sometimes after the darkness fell, other men would drift by from the town but they would see his easel leaning against the shack and keep walking along the beach, not wanting or daring to annoy him.

One day he took her with him to the art shop located in a short, strip mall beside the big Hilton Hotel. There he introduced her to Williard, a little bald Brit who had started the strip mall some twenty years before when they were first building the big new tourist hotels. Most of the tourists did not go very far from the hotels, so it was lucky for his new mall that he had built close to the hotels and that they were successful and grew in number.

She said to Williard that she would like to have a tourist store in his mall. He glanced at Charlie and smiled at them and said "I would be pleased to have your store here, but you must know that it takes a lot of money. First you must have the money for the rent and a deposit. Then there will be a need to fix up your space and buy some shelves and goods to sell. It takes quite an investment to start a store."

That night when she was home alone in her hut, she pulled out the coconut shells and counted up the money and tried to figure how long it would be before she would have enough to start a small store. Based on what Williard had told her, she had more than half what she needed. The trouble was that her savings were no longer growing. Since Charlie had come, her regular business had stopped and she didn't want it to start up again.

Charlie continued to paint her picture, but now they both knew that it was taking too long, for he had redone her face and her eyes many times. He would not let her look at the painting. Finally, one morning while he painted she could see that he was unusually quiet and then he said the words she didn't want to hear but had feared all along he was going to say. "The sugar boat is coming tomorrow."

"Take me with you," she said.

"I'll be back. I just need to make some business arrangements. To get some money from the paintings they are selling for me in Bridgetown and do a few other things. Then I'll be back. I promise."

"If you leave, you'll never be back."

He stayed with her during the night and when the sun came up, he arose and slowly gathered his things together and they walked up the beach together. She waited while the boat left the harbor and watched until it faded below the horizon.

It was only a week later that she began to feel sick in the mornings. A doctor in town who had sometimes visited her in the night told her that she was healthy, but that if she wanted to make sure the baby was healthy, she had better change her line of work. Charlie had left her some money, but she knew it would not last long, so she bought a nice looking, loosely fitting dress and fixed her hair up and went to Williard and asked him if she could help him in the art store. He told her that she could come in two or three evenings a week and help to clean up and dust the paintings and perhaps wait on customers that came in while he was busy. She started that night and, in this way, managed to live without using up too much of her savings.

She continued to live in her little shack and now the neighborhood boys did not even tease her, because they were afraid that Charlie might come back, such was the impression he had made on them. Sometimes, they would even bring her fresh fruit from town and offer it respectfully to her if she was home or else leave it carefully on her doorstep.

Thus did she live as the months passed. Each time the sugar boat came, she would run to the wharf and watch it dock, but Charlie was never on it. Once, Williard called her to the back office after the mail delivery and passed her a small package. She ran with it to her small hut and lay on the settee and slowly opened it and took out the American dollars it contained. She walked back to the store and asked Williard to read the letter to her. Charlie had taken some paintings from Bridgetown up to Tortolla, but was expecting to be back as soon as he finished some paintings he was doing in the Virgin Islands.

Such was Conchita's luck that the fall she had her baby was one of the worst hurricane seasons in recent history. By mid October, there had already been many storms when Lana started as a squall off the coast of Guyana and then headed westward over Trinidad and across the Caribbean. Through Trinidad, it cut a swath of destruction and headed straight for San Cristobel on its way to Honduras. Within a matter of hours, the realization grew among the population that they were in for a mauling.

Williard told Conchita the storm was coming and that she would be safer in the basement of the store, which was storm-proofed. Then he went out to help the neighboring store-owners board up their windows and doors. As the winds began to scream, she worried more and more about her treasure stored in the coconut shells and, since Williard was out, she decided to go to her hut.

As she struggled along the beach, the winds had grown stronger than she had thought. The tall coconut trees swayed and twisted dangerously over her head and the surf was pounding on the beach with great cracks like the old cannon they fired on festival day. Several times she fell down as she fought the raging torment, but she managed to make her way to the little hut. It was still standing when she arrived, but denuded of all its periphery, like the wall she had placed outside, and the chairs and even the stairs. The main door was smashing against the wall and loosening on its hinges.

She managed to crawl inside the door and pull the inside latch to stop it from bashing the wall. Then she huddled on her cot. The wind was shrieking ferociously through the windows and walls and the little hut shook on the stakes driven into the ground. After gaining back some of her breath, she crawled over to the corner and drew out the coconut shells and placed them on the cot. As she did so, she could feel pains growing in her abdomen and she lay on the cot and knew instinctively that the contractions were coming very close together.

The world around her howled in mighty protest and the pain from within grew in its intensity until it merged with the storm. Lost in the vast turmoil, she hardly heard the individual sounds. The smashing of the walls tearing from the foundation stakes. The roof lifting off into the turbulent void. The splintering crash of the hut finally leaving the foundation. As the strong contractions pulled together one after the other, she was only dimly conscious of driving rain and gales. Then came a scream followed by a small cry heard by no one amidst the mighty scale of nature's fury.

The storm raged for most of the night and in the early morning Williard returned from the store in which he had been trapped and roamed the basement of the art shop looking for her. It was not long until he realized that she must have gone to her little hut, although he could not imagine why, so he made his way along the beach to the place where it had been. But only the broken stakes remained and all else had been washed up amongst the coconut trees. He found her body sheltered under the overturned settee beneath the trees, clutching a blanket, and then he heard a wail and in the folds of the blanket, he found a small naked baby, miraculously alive, which he quickly bundled up and carried to his house by the store. Then he asked around town and obtained the help of a women who sometimes worked for him in the store. She took a room in his house that very day and arranged it conveniently for her and the baby. The next day, Williard mailed a letter to the Barbados.

A month later, the sugar boat from Barbados arrived at the big government wharf and a tall strong looking man strode off carrying some sticks and cases and proceeded directly to the big hotel across the street. A short while later, he walked down to the beach and towards the large tourist hotels in the distance. He paused for a time at a spot where some small stakes stood in a square at the edge of the beach and then he continued along to the art shop in the strip mall by the Hilton Hotel.

Williard took him up to the house where a pleasant-looking, middle-aged, woman cuddled a little baby girl with dark eyes. And then Charlie took a painting out of his big case and set it on the table against the wall for

Williard and his housekeeper to see. It was of a young, dark-faced woman reclining on a fine sofa in a living room with a window behind her. Through the window could be seen a large square rigger rounding a point of land on a gently rolling ocean and heading into the bay. She was dressed in a pretty pink dress and wore a gold bracelet on her arm that lay on her hip. Her eyes were gentle and loving and seemed to be watching anyone who was looking at the picture.

"For the little one when she grows up," he said.

"She is very beautiful," said the woman.

Charlie left after a few days for Jamaica, with a wanderer's look in his eyes, saying he knew a fine place in the Blue Mountains where he could make some good paintings. He said he would send some samples down in the spring. Williard shook his head and offered the woman a permanent position.

For many months afterwards, there were reports that the young boys from the town were finding American dollars along the beach. People thought the money must have floated in from a ship that had passed by during the storm, or been lost by a tourist who had been caught in the turmoil and sought shelter in the coconut groves. The boys used the money to buy rum from the bartenders at the back door of the hotel until gradually it ran out and they could find no more.

VIRTUAL REALITY

He moves silently to the basement on booted feet, spurs jingling quietly. The gun is hanging on a wall beside a tool cabinet. He takes it into his hands and hefts it lovingly, spins it and points it around the room, pulling the trigger and clicking the hammer. It is a beautiful revolver, silver plated with a pearl handle and entwined ropes engraved on the barrel. On one side of the handle are two notches, worn smooth but still visible.

He grasps a handful of cartridges from a can. The shiny brass-cased shells fit perfectly in the cylinder and when he snaps it shut, the lead points of the bullets fill the round hollows of the chambers. He spins the cylinder and it seems heavier and more solid. He points the gun towards a large wooden beam at the other end of the basement and squeezes the trigger. The basement seems to explode with noise and fire and smoke and the gun jumps so hard he bangs his hand on a water pipe. As the smoke thins out, he can see that a large chunk has been blown out of the beam.

Excitedly, he leans an old mattress against the wall and stands a sheet of plywood in front of it and then lines up a row of cans in front of the plywood. He fires at the cans from the hip and watches in fascination as they fly back against the plywood, each with a neat hole in the middle. George Walters, balding, 5 foot two, one hundred ten pounds, is a very good shot. He doesn't understand why. He is amazed. This is the first time he has ever fired a gun.

In the next room, his computer hums quietly, throwing its colored light into the darkness. George often works at home on his programs. Ten years ago, he graduated from university with a computer science degree, majoring in programming. Now, he is into multimedia, producing CD disks from snatches of video, music and text that enable the user to participate in the experiences he creates. He has won awards for his work, especially those designed for young people to learn about different eras by simulating and participating in them.

The litter of his current project lies scattered around the room. An old record collection - Gene Autry, Marty Robbins and the like. Old videos of western movies. They feature lone riders in barren lands. Showdowns in dusty deserted streets. Bank robbers scrambling for their horses and snapping shots at roof tops.

George found the gun hanging on a wall behind the cash register in a small general store on a highway between Wichita and Kansas City where he had stopped for gas on the way home from vacation.

"Is that for sale?" he asked the round, red-faced storekeeper.

The storekeeper glanced backwards. "A hundred bucks and it's yours."

George threw five twenties on the counter. Suddenly, the storekeeper smiled. "It's an authentic gun from the old west," he said. I bought it out in Arizona at an old ranch auction. They said it was owned by a gambler who was killed in a saloon fight."

Jane, George's wife, is not happy about the gun. She believes that no good comes from guns. Jane is a lawyer and has had some first hand experience on the matter. She is a successful lawyer and travels a lot, leaving George plenty of time alone. He is often lonesome, but is not very social, so he loses his loneliness in his work. He and Jane live in a big old farm house just outside the city. It is more than a century old, with walls two feet thick and stone fireplaces in every room. It is on a very large treed lot, with the original stone walls around the boundaries. Jane loved the house when they first saw it one crisp Saturday afternoon in the fall when they were out for a drive and saw the "open house" sign. She wrote a cheque for the down payment on the spot.

The gun has hung in the basement for a week. Only today, he took the time to buy some bullets for it. Today, while Jane is away on a trip, he places the cans upright in a row. Then he turns his back on them and walks slowly away. Suddenly, he drops down almost on one knee and spins around, all the while drawing the gun. In a flash, he fires and the center can flies backwards against the wall. He aims by instinct. He is fast. A natural.

He sets up match sticks as targets by wedging them into a crack in a board laid in front of the plywood sheet. He hits them every time and soon he is firing two shots at each, the first to graze the white tip of the match and light it and the second shot to put out the flame. He does this by drawing and firing, shoving the gun into it's holster and then drawing and firing again. Images fill his mind - of Clint Eastwood and John Wayne, of High Noon and the OK Corral. George Walters gets into what he does. That night, he works until dawn on his interactive program.

He walks down the middle of the dusty street, a tall stranger dressed in black approaching him. He walks slowly forward, barely breathing. His heart pounds as he waits for a sign - a sudden squint, a jerking of the hand hovering over the forty-five. The stranger stops. The hand edges closer to the weapon. He waits until the hand starts a sudden move. When it does, he draws and fires in a single fluid motion. He feels the buck of the pistol grip against his palm. Sees the stranger drop into the dirt - the relieved townspeople flooding into the streets.

He bought a holster when he bought the cartridges. First he went to the bank to pick up the money he needed. He always went to the same teller, a plump, young, auburn-haired woman named Stephanie. If she was busy, he would always wait until she was free, waving other waiting customers to go ahead of him. He liked to kid with her. And she always had a big smile for him.

"How you doing, today, Steph", he would say.

"Well, if it isn't Georgie", she would reply.

Then they were into little quips about how Jane had better watch out or some girl would steal him or "Give me all the money and we'll fly away to a desert isle". They have known each other for years. But this is their only relationship. If they met outside the bank, George would not know what to say. George has few relationships. And they are very contained. Each in their own neat compartment.

He headed with his money to a police equipment store a couple of blocks away. There, he looked over the collection of holsters and asked the clerk which one would fit an old western colt forty-five.

"We don't get much call for those", said the clerk.

"The gun's a collector's item," said George. "Once belonged to a gunfighter."

The clerk rummaged around for a while and came up with a brown, leather-tooled holster. "I think you're in luck. This one should fit. And I got a deal for you. It's been around for a while, so you can have it for fifty dollars."

George paid the man and went back to the office. That afternoon, he left early and hurried home and downstairs and buckled the holster on. Then he slid the gun into it and could see that it would do very well. All it needed was a little oil, which he quickly dug out of a drawer and worked into the leather. Then he eased the gun in and out a few times and began to draw. And point. And back into the holster. And out and pointing and back. It quickly became fluid motion. Simple beauty. Art.

There is an eerie calm as he treads softly in the dim light. Only the squeak of his leather boots is heard. He moves cautiously, and the star on his chest glints from the occasional ray of moonlight shining through the windows. The gun swings heavily on the hip. He can smell sweaty horses and dusty corrals and he is headed for the show-down - tall and independent and strong. In control. He reaches a corner and flattens against the planks of the wall. Then he leaps a great somersault into the adjoining room, drawing and firing as he lands upright. He fans the hammer, shooting all six cans from the line-up in an explosive volley that leaves his ears ringing and his eyes burning with acrid smoke. He returns to the computer room and works long into the night.

When Jane comes back from her trips, she and George resume their normal routine. They drive to work together down the freeway and into the financial district. She drops him off in front of her office building and then he walks the remaining two blocks to his office. If she plans to work late, and she often does, she calls him and he catches the commuter train home. If she comes home early enough, they go for a walk together. Then he works on his computer and she on the papers in her briefcase.

The gun is stored in the basement, but George can't get it out of his mind, and soon he begins to put it into his briefcase when he goes to work. He is so good with it. It feels good to be so good at something. Before leaving the office at lunch-time, he slides it under his long coat. Then he walks the streets, feeling the heavy weight against his body, feeling the secret power. He begins to grow a mustache.

When hunting season starts in October, he walks in the early mornings up the back lane and into the woods.

He carries his hunting rifle as usual, but also has the forty-five under his coat in its holster. Sometimes he draws and fires and feels the bucking power in his hand. Once a rabbit bounds out of the bush in front of him he draws the gun in a flash and shoots it before it has taken two hops. He shoots it in the head and it falls in the road with hardly a twitch.

There are killer-thieves at large in the countryside. The Marshall stalks them in the back roads near the town. His boots crunch softly in the frost, carefully avoiding the crisp newly-fallen red leaves. There is a jingle of silver spurs. His long white coat hangs open revealing the occasional flash of a silver gun. His wide Stetson is pulled low on his forehead. And his shadow is tall in the morning sun. His face is a grim mask with steel grey eyes that dart sideways towards the darkest shadows. It is a thin line between the law and the lawless in these times. Only the killers survive. Only the best. He snaps off the computer and sits back. Takes a deep breath.

Next day. High noon. There is the thump of tooled riding boots on board sidewalks. The jingle of spurs. The snorting of hastily tethered horses. The smell of dust stirring in the street. The squeak of rusty door hinges. The weight of a Colt 45 swinging on a lean hip. The startled faces of tellers and bank customers. The 45 in the hand, so fast that no-one sees the move. The gasp of recognition from behind the counter.

"My God, what are you doing?"

A barked command splits the silence, "Lie down!" The voice is husky with emotion, punctuated by the click of the hammer being pulled back.

People scramble to the floor. A young man starts to cry. A woman screams into her hands. Most people close their eyes. Some of them sneak quick glances sideways. They are scattered in all directions and positions, like a giant hand had swept across the room.

George Walters throws a canvas bag at the frightened young teller. He mimics a slow West Texas drawl. "Fill it up, Steph. And make it fast." She moves from drawer to drawer, grabbing whatever is in them with shaking hands, stuffing the bag. In a nearby office, a man pushes a button and waits, staying out of sight. A video camera whirs silently in a corner near the ceiling. George assumes a dramatic pose, legs spread wide, thumb hooked in his jeans pocket. He waves the gun at her and drawls "Snap it up, Steph."

He steps outside into the bright sunshine and looks for the hitching rails. There are flashing red lights in the street. He fires a couple of quick shots at a movement on the roof across the street and takes cover in the doorway.

A couple of blocks up the street, Jane leaves her office building and heads towards the bank for some spending money before the lunch-time rush. As she strolls down the street, she can see a commotion in front of the bank and some policemen stringing a rope across the street to hold the pedestrians back.

George runs back into the bank where some of the people are starting to get up and fires a shot at the ceiling. He orders Stephanie to come around the counter and stand beside him. He grabs her by the arm and half drags her to the front entrance. A voice on a loudspeaker tells him to put his hands up and come out.

Jane reaches the police barrier where a crowd has gathered. She can see the bank quite clearly now.

The bank robber and his prey step into the street. Jane gasps. A policeman yells "He's got a hostage." A plan swings into action. A sniper on the roof shifts imperceptibly and lines up the cross hairs of his scope, keeping an eye on the police captain at the corner with his arm raised. The captain lowers his arm. The sniper squeezes the trigger.

The bank robber is slammed against the wall of the bank like a puppet whose strings have been yanked. Jane stands frozen in the street, unable to move. A policeman says "Move on, everyone. It's all over. Go on about your business." Jane screams.

The horses pull and rear on the hitching rails. The Marshall in blue leans down and shakes his head. His badge glints in the noonday sun. There are gunmen standing on the roof. Rifles pointing into the sky. Blood running into the dust. Relieved townspeople flooding into the streets.

CITY BOY

Jake came silently through the kitchen door. I didn't hear him until he was inside. I went quietly to the door and saw him standing there in the dark with his rifle in his hand holding it under the stock near the scope and the shoulder strap hanging down. I had been waiting for almost an hour since I called, watching for Jake and also keeping track of the dark movements in the field in back of the house.

"I saw him," said Jake.

"You know where he is?" I asked redundantly.

"How do you get to the upstairs window?"

"You can't shoot from there. You'll scare the hell out of Mary."

"Is she sleeping?"

"Yeah."

"How about the patio. Can we get out there?"

"The door makes a noise when it slides. But we can try. Just make sure you don't shoot the neighbours."

We move quietly through the shadows of the family room. Election results are on the television. The Liberals are losing. Jake holds his gun pointed carefully to the floor. I move the security bar and slide the door slowly. It grates, but the dark spot in the back yard stays calmly in the same place, feeding on something. I move the outside screen door carefully. We both look out. Jake walks carefully outside into the cool night air. He kneels beside the barbecue and takes careful aim. He takes his time.

The gun makes a loud pop, reverberates briefly and then there is silence.

The spot flops once and then is still.

Jake stands up and walks casually back towards the door.

"Got him," he says.

"Did you get him?" I ask.

"He's dead."

"How do you know?"

"Oh I killed him. He'll be dead in the morning for sure."

"You're pretty damn confident about it."

"Yeah, I got him all right."

"That was a good shot. You're a good shot."

"I could only find one bullet."

"Good thing you made good use of it."

"Where's the shell case?" he asks.

"It flipped out on the deck."

We look around, but it's not there. I say, "I think it fell between the cracks."

Jake looks out into the darkness. The spot is still lying there, near a tree. "I wanted to gut shoot him. Then he'd crawl away and die somewhere else."

I was glad he made a clean kill. Jake puts his rifle down on the barbecue and walks carefully to the dark spot. He stops about ten yards away and looks. Then he comes back. "Got a flashlight?"

"Yeah. Just a second." I go inside and return a moment later with the flashlight and give it to Jake."

"There could be another one," he says.

He goes back out and shines the light on the spot. It lies still. Jake goes closer. Touches it with his boot. I go stand beside him.

"Yeah. He's dead." "What's that beside him?"

"Dead skunk."

"Coyotes eat skunks?"

"Yeah, they'll eat anything."

"I don't smell anything."

"He probably didn't get a chance to spray."

"What in hell am I going to do with them?"

"Oh, just throw them into the hay field. The crows'll get 'em. Pick 'em clean"

I'm doubtful, thinking of the neighbour on that side and his six kids. "I don't know."

"Well, take 'em down by the river and throw 'em in the bushes."

"Yeah, that's a good idea. Not in the river though."

"No, jeeze, no. Not in the river."

We walk back towards the house in the dark. Jake yells "Hey, Look out."

I jump and he laughs with delight.

"You bugger," I say.

Then I comment, "That's a fairly quiet gun."

"It's a twenty-two magnum."

"A magnum, eh? I'm going to get a shotgun. For birds. I could have got him myself."

"Awful noisy. A friend of mine fired his shotgun at night and six Mountie cars showed up in his yard."

"Six. Holy jeeze. Maybe I should get a twenty-two."

"Ah, you won't need it that much. There shouldn't be that many pests around."

"I saw two deer while I was waiting for you."

"Two deer. Where?" He looks interested.

I point up the hill across the road. "Don't shoot them though."

He says, "I better go home."

We get into my new Buick. He points the muzzle of his rifle to the floor. We head across the river and turn up the back road to his house.

He says, "I saw a bear running across here the other day."

"A bear." This is directly in back of our house, just across the river.

"Yeah, a small one. Ran across the road and into the trees."

When I return home, I can smell them in the driveway and then I can smell them inside the house. I wonder if we did the right thing leaving them there. In the morning, I take the bodies down by the river in a wheelbarrow and bury them near the bushes.

A SAD AND BEAUTIFUL DANCE

Alexander brings to the table two shot glasses and a bottle of Polish vodka and sits down with a huge sigh. He is grey and balding and walks with a stoop in his shoulders. Freda, his round, rosy wife, follows with some heavy whole-wheat bread on a cutting board and a roll of kolbassa. Alexander cuts thick slices of meat and begins breaking the bread with his hands, stuffing small chunks into his mouth and rinsing with the vodka. All the while, he is talking.

We are sitting at the dining room table of a large house in the Humber area of Toronto. There is an ornate walnut dining room suite in the room and on the wall above the hutch there are several old black and white photos of family members. Two large leaded windows on the opposite side of the room overlook a flower garden.

"Last night I heard the knock again. There was no one. It was in my head, you understand? But it was real, too."

"It will always be real to him," says Freda.

I chew the meat and bread and drink the strong vodka and listen. The meat is fresh and firm and tasty. The garlic assaults the taste buds on my tongue. It is tangy and strong.

I come here once every month to pay my rent. Alexander and Freda own several fine houses in Toronto, something they started when they immigrated after the Second World War. They scraped up the money to buy a duplex. He worked two jobs for several years, sixteen hours a day, while she cleaned floors and did washing for people in the affluent areas of Forest Hills and Rosedale. They rented the other half of the duplex and used the money to pay the mortgage. Eventually, they extended this holding into several houses. Now they are retired.

Each time I come to pay the rent, he invites me in. We have a couple of shot glasses of his good Polish vodka and talk. It was mostly small talk at first, but gradually the talk became more personal and we both began to look forward to the visits. "He likes you," said Freda.

He has seldom talked about the old country. It is only recently that he has talked about the dreams.

"The knock is three hard raps in a row, then a pause, then three more. They go on until I am fully awake. The knocks are very insistent, sharp, but hard enough to rattle the door. Then I see my brother standing there staring at me."

"My brother was very strong. He was taller than you, more than six feet, and thicker. But you look like Jorge. Don't you think so, Freda? Doesn't he look like Jorge?" Alexander has been saying this since I first met him.

Freda nods as she always does. "Blue eyes, curly hair. Yes, just like Jorge". She points to one of the pictures on the wall. The resemblance is startling. I wonder if it would be better if I stopped coming here - stopped raising these painful memories for my friend.

Alexander continues, "He was the most powerful man I have ever seen. And he liked to show off his strength. Sometimes, he would walk to the front of the car if you were sitting in it and grab it by the bumper and pick it up and then rock it up and down and laugh. Yes, that's right, by the front bumper. He could lift it quite high, even with people in it.

"He didn't fight with people, but he liked to show off. Sometimes he would grab people who were acting up in the bar and hold them against the wall and they wouldn't be able to move. He was like a lot of big men - a peace-maker.

"One night, he was in the bar when two SS soldiers burst through the door and began to rough up some of the people who were there. When they hit his friend, he grabbed the soldiers and pinned them against the bar. Of course, they were armed, but when they tried to reach for a pistol, Jorge just tightened his grip and they could not move.

"He held them like that for what seemed like a long time because he knew he had acted impulsively and that when he let them go, they would probably kill him. Even if he managed to get away, they would hunt him down. They always killed people who showed too much resistance, especially if it was done in public. Then two more soldiers walked into the bar and pulled out their pistols and put them against his head. He let go and they took him away.

"It was later that night that I heard the knock. Freda and I were in our bed and Henri, he was just a baby then, was sleeping beside us. I went to the door and when I opened it, four soldiers swarmed in. They had a madness in their eyes and they were rowdy and they said I had five minutes to dress and go with them. I had no choice. I didn't know what they wanted with me. But it wasn't me. They said my brother had asked to see me. Then they all laughed. I will never forget that night.

Alexander stops talking and stares at the floor. In the silence, I begin to talk about my guitar playing and how it started with my brother-in-law, Harold. I tell them that he came to visit Julie and me. He wanted to start a career in the restaurant business. First, he was going to stay a long time. Then he found out he needed some formal training and so he gave up and went back home. He left his guitar behind to cover his board. It was a classical guitar but it was cheap and battered and had a dull, flat sound. It just sat in a corner of the family room for months.

"You should play for us sometime. I think you would play very well." says Freda.

I tell them how I began.

"Every day on the way to the subway station I walk by Harvey's Music Store."

Alexander nods and manages a small smile.

"I saw a sign in the window. It said 'Guitar Lessons', and I thought of the old guitar and how I wanted to play it. So I went inside."

"I found Harvey sitting at the back of the store behind a glass counter filled with items like guitar picks, tuning forks and drumsticks. He was a neat little man with round rim glasses and a little white fringe of hair. I later learned that he played and taught most of the instruments in the shop. When I walked in, he was playing a classical guitar, holding it in the classical style with its body resting on his knee, and the long fingernails of his right hand plucking the strings in a slow tune I later learned was a Spanish dance. I was captivated by the clear, mournful tones and stopped and listened inside the door. I had never heard a classical guitar played in person before. It was the most beautiful sound I had ever heard."

I select another slice of Kolbassa and chew it slowly. Alexander and Freda wait silently for me to continue.

"After a few moments, the old man paused and looked up and I said I had noticed the sign in the window and wanted to ask about guitar lessons."

"So he says 'And what kind of music would you like to play?' and I say 'classical, I guess. I have a classical guitar and I always liked classical music' and he says 'Have you had any musical training?' and I say 'No.' and he says 'We can start with the basics and I say 'That's cool'. We set the time for Thursday evenings from seven to eight. Five dollars a session.

"So I started that week and while I was there, I bought an elementary guitar book which began with individual notes and scales and simple tunes and finally worked up to a few Chopin melodies. When I arrived home that night, I started working on the book right away."

Alexander gets a far-away look in his eyes as he listens and pours another glass of vodka.

"Jorge used to play the harmonica. He never took lessons, but he made good music for us. He used to play and dance and stamp his big feet so hard the house shook. The children would laugh and dance around him in circles."

As I leave, Freda says "The dreams will stop after a while. Next time you come, bring Julie. Say hello to her for us."

"OK," I lie.

Julie and I were married about five years ago. We rent a floor of their biggest house, close to High Park and backing on a wooded ravine. It has three stories and its own driveway, as well as a big sunporch stretching across the entire back of the house and overlooking the ravine. The old guitar leans in a corner of the sunporch.

I love the sunporch and often spend time there. I sit there alone with my coffee after dinner and gaze out into the ravine. The sunporch has polished maple floors covered with rag scatter rugs and filled with wicker furniture we bought at a flea market. The woods are deep and green with maples and poplars along the edge, and far down I can see tall willows beside the stream that runs through the ravine on its course to the flat land, under the Gardiner Expressway and into the murky waters of Lake Ontario. When the evenings become warm in the early summer, I open the windows and feel a breeze coming up from the lake and smell the musty freshness of the woods. It is quiet and peaceful.

I go to pay the rent on the first of every month. Sometimes I find a reason to visit between rent days. This time it is for permission to paint the windows in the sunporch.

"You can paint them," says Alexander, "but you must pay for the paint. And don't get any of it on the windows. If you do, scrape it all off with a razor blade."

I sip the vodka and smile. I know he will pay for the paint when the job is done.

When I go back to the house, Julie is out somewhere as always. I start to move the furniture around in the sunporch and then notice the old guitar in the corner. I haven't played it since I bought my new hand-made one, so I pick it up, sit down and let my mind wander back through the twists and turns of the forest of memories.

I made a lot of progress taking lessons from Harvey. No question about that. I started with the book I had bought and before long, I was picking out tunes. I especially liked some of the Beatles tunes. Of course I didn't sound anything like the Beatles, but eventually you could recognize the tunes. And gradually, they became smoother and I could play them without looking at the music.

The first winter with Harvey, I kept up the lessons, and worked through some introductory books, as well as several music sheets that he gave me. By spring, Harvey was saying that I was making good progress - better than most of his other students. He taught me the slow, beautiful dance I had heard him play that first day. It became my favourite and I played it over and over.

I buried myself more and more in the guitar, playing virtually all the time I was home, and even taking the guitar to work and playing it at noon and sometimes during breaks. I also got a job playing at a restaurant in the evenings. This gave me lots of practice, and I could even earn some extra money. That's where I got the money to buy the new guitar. A hand-made one that Harvey had to order in from Spain.

The sunporch became a music studio. It contained a mahogany music stand, a special foot rest to keep my knee at just the right height for resting the guitar as I played and a stool designed especially for classical guitar players. Scattered around the room was a variety of tuning equipment and sheet music and music books.

In addition to my regular practice sessions, I often played for hours at a time. I was now into Bach, trying just about everything of his that was available for the guitar. I mastered the Cello Suites, adapted for the guitar and I would sit in the porch and play their sharp bouncy melodies. Sometimes Julie would be working in the garden hearing the music and recognizing its beauty but probably trying to block it out.

As I progressed well with my guitar I began to feel that I needed a better teacher, with a more advanced program. I had been talking to other students and friends who said that I should study at the Conservatory to learn the guitar properly.

I visited the Conservatory and looked through their calendars and the brochures. Later, while trying to decide which program to follow, I noticed an ad in the Star saying that a Conservatory teacher was giving lessons in her home in the evenings. I phoned her as soon as I got back to the office. That was how I met Anna.

She was a few years older than me and told me that she needed the money from the lessons because she had been recently divorced. Although she grew up in Philadelphia, she had studied guitar for many years, both in Toronto and in Granada. Her dream was to return to Spain to study. Anna was quiet spoken and intelligent and played for me when I first went to her house. Her delicate, finely-shaped fingers could fly over the strings, and she made the guitar sound like an orchestra. The first day I met her, I thought she was beautiful when she leaned over her guitar, with her long brown hair draped over her shoulder. I signed up for weekly lessons. Before long, Anna told me that if I kept improving, I could soon give concerts.

Each week I was the last student of the day. Anna held the lessons in her living room by the fireplace. She made a crackling fire before I arrived and after the half hour lesson was complete, we played duets together. Then we had coffee by the fire and talked, sometimes for hours.

As I think about these things I am playing the Spanish dance in the sunporch with my eyes closed and gently swaying on my stool and my thoughts return to Julie. Who knows what came first? Did I replace her with the guitar or did she find her new friend first? It's hard for me to put an order to it now. Maybe it all happened together. It's true I fell in love with the music. At first I didn't know it would take so much time, but it did and then I was in love all over again. I gained a love and lost a lover.

Alexander stiffens when I tell him that Julie is gone. Mercifully, Freda is not there at the time. "How could this happen?" he says.

"It happens a lot nowadays," I say.

"I see these things happen, but I don't understand. You young people have so much and yet you seem to be so unhappy."

"Money doesn't buy happiness," I reply. I can't believe I have uttered this platitude. But I can't think of anything else to say. I am waiting for his response to work its way out. I hope we will stay friends. But he waits for more.

"I suppose it was the guitar. When I started playing, it was half an hour a day. Then as I got into it more, it became two hours a day and then three. She began to say it was like she was living alone. I guess that was when we separated."

Alexander is silent.

I continue, "In the past year or so, when I play my favorite pieces, they play themselves. It's as though the guitar is being played by someone else and I am the audience. I watch my hands playing and they seem to have a life of their own. The music becomes a part of me. I float and drift and sometimes, I play on and on after supper and then I realize that the sun is coming up."

Alexander sits silently for a long moment, then says "Maybe a person is only allowed so much beauty in a life."

We sit there together silently looking out into the garden.

Freda enters the room and asks, "How is Julie?"

I look at the table and say, "Julie's gone."

"Oh, did she go to visit her family? It's nice to visit your family. So many families live so far apart these days. Families should stay close. Is she staying for long?"

" I'm afraid you don't understand. She's gone for good. She's not coming back." I can feel my voice cracking, a tightness in my chest. I've had enough of this.

Freda and Alexander say nothing for a few moments. They glance at each other. I take a long drink of vodka.

Freda says "You young people have so much these days. Things we never even dreamed of in the old country.

It's sad to see so much unhappiness. It's hard to understand."

Alexander continues wistfully. "There is so much opportunity here. I wish my son Henri would have taken advantage. All he did was to buy a motorcycle and then drive it, drive it all the time. We came to this country so our children and grandchildren could have opportunity that we never had. Now they have it and don't take advantage of it. I don't understand them.

"We knew about good things, you understand. But we knew we couldn't have them. They were beyond reach. If you had a few books to put on a shelf in your living room, you were considered a rich man.

"But we were happy in our way. On Sundays we would all gather together - my mother and father and aunts and uncles and sisters and brothers and after dinner Jorge would play with the children and the men would sit and talk in the living room. Our life was hard, but we found - - -"

I shuffle my feet, wanting to stand up.

Freda says "He doesn't want to listen to this, Alex. She turns to me with a sad but sympathetic look. "Would you like some coffee, John?"

"No thanks", I manage to say. I pour some more vodka and pass the bottle to Alexander."

Later, I have some coffee on the sunporch. It is quiet and peaceful, as usual, but the house is big and lonely. The skies are gray and the woods seem as desolate as my life. I call Anna and go to her place.

She is sitting beside the fire, pushing around bits of wood with a poker to raise up the flames.

"I'm going back to Spain next month", she announces. "To Granada. I can learn so much more there, and the atmosphere is more agreeable, not to mention the climate. Why don't you come with me?"

We had talked about it during our long nights together, but it had seemed improbable and far away. Now she has decided.

"I'm not sure. I need to think. A lot has happened lately."

We talk about it long into the night. I stay at her place and by the next day we have made our plans. That night I go to give my notice to Alexander. I take my guitar with me.

Freda lets me in. "Alex is in the study", she says. She looks subdued.

When I walk into the study, Alexander is sitting brooding by a window overlooking the garden.

He looks up at me, "I saw my brother again last night. Standing by the door, facing me. After the knocks. Looking as he did when I last saw him alive. There was terrible sadness in his face. Beyond grief."

I watch him sitting there facing the window. "Perhaps it is your own sadness you see in him."

Alexander turns towards me, "There was such a terrible sadness. How is it possible?"

I have no answer, so I take out my guitar and begin to play the slow Spanish dance. The plaintive notes fill the air and carry within them all the sadness in the room, the sadness of the world. Alexander sits with his back towards me silently looking out into the garden. Freda comes to the door and listens and looks at him for a long time. Then she turns her loving gaze to me and puts a rosy-cheeked smile on her face and very slowly nods her head up and down. Her eyes are soft and moist.

A LONELY FARM IN THE FOREST

The news came that winter as we expected and towards the end, Lynn went to visit. On a mild day in late winter, when the snow was starting to melt and the winds were mellowing, I flew east for the funeral. Two weeks later, Thane's son was born and Donna took him with her back to New York to live.

We see them sometimes in the summers, those summers when we happen to visit at the same time. We drive down on the new four-lane highway and when we pass the location of the old farm, if we pay close attention, we can tell when we pass over the exact spot where the house used to be. At first when the highway was new, there were some barn-boards by the side of the road, but they gradually disappeared, and now the only way you can tell there was an old farm is if you knew it well exactly as it used to be.

The farm house was over one hundred and fifty years old and covered with vines that were so thick you could barely see out the windows. It had been kept clean enough to be habitable, but no improvements had been made for many years. The main reason for this was that the farm had been appropriated to make way for the new highway which was planned to go through the middle of the property.

The house was at the end of a long tree-lined lane that ran across a meadow and behind it was the deep forest that stretched far to the north. There was a well on the left side of the lane near the house and further to the left was a barn. Inside the house on the main floor was a kitchen, a small living room and a sitting room and upstairs there were three bedrooms.

There was an old organ in the living room, an old pump organ with worn foot pedals. I sometimes played simple tunes on it as a child but had never progressed beyond that stage. Sometimes the valves in it would stick so that if you filled the blowers with air by pumping the foot pedals, they would release hours later. Depending on how the stops had been left, it might even play two or three drawn-out notes.

During the day, the old house was very peaceful and quiet, although rather somber with the limited light that filtered through the vines. But at night, the whole character of the house would change. The darkness would take on a midnight-black intensity and even if there was only a small breeze moving, the vines would beat against the walls and windows, sometimes softly like a lover come to call and at other times loudly with a violence that spoke of fear and evil. In one moment, they would be heard on one side of the house and in the next moment, on the other. The wind, when it was strong, would shriek through the walls and the house would creak and groan.

Several other members of the family went home to visit during the summer when Thane and I stayed at the farm. Thane was Lynn's brother. Somehow, through the letters and telephone calls that formed the family's communications network, the idea of a reunion had grown. What everyone left unsaid was that they wanted to visit Thane.

There was no one place large enough to accommodate everyone and we had to use every dwelling the family had at its disposal. My parents, who lived in St. Stephen, owned the old farm and told us that we were welcome to use it as long as we could take it as we found it. People rarely stayed there anymore. There were no takers and lots of reasons why nobody at the reunion wanted to stay there. It was too far away from everyone else, being eighty kilometers into the woods on an old partly paved country road. There was nothing within fifty kilometers in any direction but wolves, coyotes and bears. And there were stories of strange and unexplained events. Lynn did not want to stay there.

But I had spent many happy summers there in my youth and was eager to find someone to stay with me for a few nights and drive back and forth each day to be with the others. After much discussion and bantering, it was Thane who decided to go with me. He said he had heard so much about the old place that he wanted to see it. We would take a few beers, wieners and rolls for the evenings and some bacon and eggs and coffee for the mornings. We would use sleeping bags and old army camp cots because the sparse bedding at the old farm would be very musty. He would cook the breakfasts and I would do the driving.

When Thane and I arrived, a storm was brewing and a wind was coming up. We opened a couple of beers and started a wood fire in the rusty stove and boiled some wieners. By the time we were eating, the rain was slashing against the sides of the house and the vines were pounding. Afterwards, I demonstrated the ancient organ, pumping the pedals and keys as hard as I could to match the howling world around us. As it grew darker, we decided to check out the bedrooms, using our flashlights because there was no electricity upstairs. We looked up the stairwell but it was very dark except for the flickering glow of the flashlights on the walls, accented by the sound of the vines and the moaning of the wind around the window casements.

Thane decided we should sleep downstairs. "This place is scary, all right," he said.

"My grandparents lived their whole lives here," I said. "It was only after they were gone that people started saying it was scary."

"Do you think it's haunted?"

"Sometimes you have to wonder," I said playfully.

We set up our camp cots in the sitting room and when we turned out the light, an impenetrable blackness enfolded us. We told each other we were holding our hands in front of our faces but couldn't see them. We lay there talking sometimes but mostly listening to the creaking, groaning, knocking turmoil around us. Sleep lingered just outside the circle of our consciousness and when it came, it was timid and shy. Mine came first because I had grown accustomed to the house. Thane might have started to drift off from time to time, but then a new noise would startle him wide awake.

After an hour or so, he arose and pulled a piece of rope out of his backpack and tied it to the string on the light bulb with the other end tied to his bunk. Every time a new noise startled him, he would reach for the rope and snap on the light without having to get out of bed. The light went on several times after that but slowly from exhaustion he fell into fitful sleep.

Later in the depths of the night, the rain stopped and the wind slowed to short gentle gusts and the fog crept silently across the forest. The vines knocked gently at times and soothingly, at least to me. I awoke to the sound of Thane turning in his cot and felt a thirst, so I arose in the dark and crept silently to the kitchen for a drink of water and found to my dismay that the old water bucket in the kitchen was empty. So my thirst became unbearable and I decided to go outside to refill the bucket from the well. I stepped gingerly in my bare feet across the wet grass and the driveway to the well and tied the bucket handle to the rope and dropped it down with a splash. As I drew the water, my attention was drawn to the dark woods around me, barely visible in the fog, and all the strange movements in the shadowy bushes. I could hear the vines tapping on the house.

Suddenly, the eerie calm was split with a shriek that seized my heart. Bent stiffly over the well and staring blindly at the foggy forest, I realized it was the old organ releasing unspent air in a wild and frantic crescendo - a fugue gone wild. This was quickly followed by a rising and high-pitched scream of terror and I saw the light of the sitting room go on. At the same time, I dropped the water bucket down the well and ran to the house. I slipped and fell face-first in the mud of the driveway, striking my nose on the rocks.

With blood running down my face and covered with mud, my pajamas torn and soiled and dripping wet I struggled to my feet and ran into the house, threw open the door with a crash and lurched into the sitting room with a shout. "Are you all right, Thane?"

He was huddled in the far corner of the room and when I appeared in the doorway, he looked up with a violent jerk. When he saw me, he opened his mouth to scream, but not a sound came forth and he simply froze in that position for a moment. It seemed to me that his eyes relaxed into a calm expression just before he fainted.

I brought some water in from the well and laid wet towels on his head and face. When he could move, I helped him to his cot and we laid on our cots in the dark and talked. The house was silent.

"Was it you?" he said, "I didn't really know it was you."

"Who did you think it was?"

"All I could think of was death."

"The organ really scared the hell out of you."

"I never want to hear that organ again. That was sheer terror. But after you came in, I don't remember anything."

We left the next day and did not return to the farm. Thane said he had seen it and that was enough. He went back to his painting and Lynn and I stayed with friends.

Thane was tall and slim and twenty-two and was a fine artist. He had learned to paint as a child during the many long days he spent in the house on his vaporizer when his asthma was bad. During attacks, he could only breathe sitting up, so at those times he would balance his easel on the bed over his legs and would stay that way for hours. By the time he got older and his asthma started to clear up, he was into the habit of painting for long periods of time. He started with water colors and then moved to oils, which he came to prefer. When he was seventeen he began to take his paintings to shows in the area and when he began to sell them, there was no question in anyone's mind about what he planned to do with his life.

When he graduated from high school, he studied for a couple of years at an art college in New York where he met and married Donna and was doing well when suddenly he gave it up and they moved back home. People were surprised at first, although those closest to him knew that he had not been feeling well and that his illnesses had become so frequent that Donna had finally talked him into going to the doctor. Word of the diagnosis spread quickly.

At that time, he didn't look any different really. He was slim and pale, but then, he had always been that way. A stranger who looked at him would see a frail young man, but what we saw was the Thane we knew, and frail was not how we would have described him. We saw a strong and lively spirit, only a new and different expression had crept into his eyes.

When we prepared to leave for our night at the farm, we had to go to his apartment to pick up some clothes. It was a two bedroom apartment and the extra bedroom had been set up as a studio. "Until the baby - - -", Donna started to say and then stopped herself when she realized what she was saying. Thane knew she was pregnant, of course. She had told him the same night he had told her about the diagnosis. She had told him her news first, otherwise, she often thought afterwards, she wouldn't have known how to tell him.

While Thane gathered his clothes, I looked around the studio at the dozens of paintings of all sizes. There were country landscapes, coastal scenes, street scenes of various cities and some portraits. Some of the later paintings from New York seemed to have more people in them than the earlier works. They featured portraits ranging from ragged and weather-beaten street people to fat and arrogant executives. Most of the subjects were smiling, as though at a camera. I remembered that Thane liked to paint from photographs. That way, he could snap a scene and take it home and avoid long exposures to the elements. Often, he would go back and shoot the same scene many times, under different conditions - morning, night, in bright sunlight and in the rain. I often told him he reminded me of Monet with his lily pond and churches. He told me he was an admirer of Monet. "To remind myself," he said, "that things are not always what they seem."

There was an unfinished oil on the easel. It was a portrait of a young woman with long, red hair flared out around her head and eyes that were round and encircled with dark rings. Her mouth was shaped in what I first thought might have been a scream. Even though the portrait was unfinished, it appeared to me at first as a powerful expression of despair. But there was more than that in her eyes and I was trying to understand her eyes when Thane re-entered the room.

"I think I have everything," he said.

"Remarkable painting," I replied as I turned to face him. "What's it mean?"

"Oh, it's something I just had to get on the canvas. But she isn't finished yet. I've been working on her so much she almost seems like an old friend." Then he looked at me with a wry chuckle. "Maybe when she's finished, I'll sit down in front of her and toast her with a glass of wine and say 'Well, here I am and here you are. What do we do now?"

We walked down to the car together.

BEFORE THE SUN GOES DOWN

Jim and Debbie have driven north into the Alps from Nice, taking the back roads and stopping occasionally to view the spectacular scenery. After driving for a few hours, they stop by the roadside overlooking a wide valley and sit on a rock lunching on fresh bread and cheese and bottled Evian water. Far below, they can see trees and farms that look like little toys.

After lunch, they drive through a construction area on the edge of a high cliff. The workers guide them carefully around the equipment and rock piles. Jim likes the winding roads and is starting to drive a little too fast. Debbie is holding onto her seat because she is afraid of heights and is sitting on the side of the car that overlooks the valley. Every time she looks out almost straight down into the deep valley her heart skips a beat.

As they drive higher into the mountains, little clumps of snow appear along the edge of the road and soon they are driving between high snow banks. When they reach the pass over the highest point in the mountains, they find that it is closed. Even if they could push through the snow, which they can't, it would be too dangerous to try to go down the other side of the mountain. So they turn around and head back.

When they get back to the construction area, the little blue Renault screeches to a stop in front of the barrier that blocks the road. Jim and Debbie just sit there in the car for a moment and look at each other. It is past quitting time, and the workmen have left for the day and closed the road. According to the map, it is the only road into this part of the mountains. Jim and Debbie are trapped. All day, they have seen no inns or hotels or anyplace else to stay. There are ski chalets, but it is off season, and they all appear to be closed.

"We can sleep in the car", says Debbie.

"It's too small" he answers, "Let's go back and check that village we passed on the way in. Maybe we can stay there for the night."

When they drive into the little village, they see a man walking to his car and pull over beside him. Jim asks, in his halting French, if there is anyplace to stay for the night. The man shakes his head. "However", he says as he points south, "there is another road out of the mountains if you go back that way. But make sure you go through before the sun goes down."

They thank him and as they drive away, the man calls "Remember, before the sun goes down."

Trying to follow the half-understood directions, they find a small likely-looking road and follow it. Almost immediately they are heading up a very steep incline and a series of switchbacks, with the road getting narrower as they drive along.

Again, Debbie is on the side looking down into the valley most of the time. After half an hour, the road ends suddenly at a large rock face. With the light beginning to fade, Jim quietly turns the car around and they head back down to the main road. Debbie says "Lets sleep in the car." Why don't we?"

"We should be able to get out", he says. "The man said there was a road. We must be able to find it."

Neither one speaks as they head down and Jim is driving a little faster. Debbie's fear grows as they swerve on the switchbacks and she feels her stomach starting to churn.

Back on the road, they turn south again and drive all the way back to the construction barrier without seeing another road. But this time, there are other cars and a truck and men are standing around talking. Jim pulls up beside them and gets out of the car.

He can't understand them very well, but relates the problem as best he can. One of the men nods understandingly and waves for Jim to follow as he climbs into the truck and starts back up the road. Jim gets into the Renault and pulls out behind the truck.

They drive for about a kilometer and then turn off into a lane towards a farm. Around the farmhouse and through a gate in the fence, there is a small road, little more than two ruts in the ground, and they follow it across a field. The grade beside them quickly becomes steeper, and soon they are driving on the edge of a very high cliff. The air is thin and clear and the valley floor is far, far below.

Now the road is covered with loose stone and is partly washed out. They stop to allow some goats to pass. In front of them is a small ditch full of muddy water running across the road, and spurting out into the wide, empty space of the valley. Several meters of the road are washed out on both sides of the ditch. Well, the truck got through, thinks Jim. He throws the car into gear and as they pull through the mud, the rear end of the car swings sideways, but then the tires hit some rocks and the car straightens out. The rocks follow the water into the empty space.

The truck is getting ahead of them, since they had stopped for the goats. It is obvious the driver knows the road well. Jim steps on the accelerator to keep the truck in sight. It is almost dark and they can hardly see the road so they are thankful for the lights of the truck ahead of them.

Debbie is so terrified her body is stiff as a board beside him, her rump suspended above her seat. She is crying and trying not to look out or down. Jim sees how upset she is, but is trying to concentrate on driving. The tires of the Renault are horribly close to the edge.

The terror grows and feeds on itself and Debbie feels it will never end, but then after a long time she opens her eyes and catches a glimpse of the valley floor which is much closer. Suddenly, the truck brakes and takes a sharp left turn onto a paved highway. They know instinctively it is the highway they had traveled earlier in the day. They are safe!

As Jim wheels the car onto the paved road, he breathes a deep sigh and sees an arm waving good-bye out of the truck speeding off into the darkness.

"Go through before the sun goes down," mutters Jim. Debbie sits with her face in her hands.

They are quiet for a while and after his adrenaline slows down, Jim's thoughts turn to Debbie. He wants to say something, but decides he'd better give it a little time. She is gathering herself together, trying to control her breathing and shivering.

Then her mood changes. "You asshole. When in hell are you going to grow up?"

He is startled and glances sideways. The fear in her face is completely gone. Instead he is drawn to her round dark eyes, fiery and piercing like twin cannons spewing out flaming steel balls.

"Uh, well, it wasn't that bad, was it? I kind of ---""Have you any idea how scared I was up there? Do you understand what it was like sitting there by the edge of a cliff in a car that someone else is driving. You have no control. You don't know from one minute to the next whether you're going to live or die. You just don't know. Can you understand that? What that feels like?"

"I don't uh ---"

"All I could think of up there was Mandy becoming an orphan. Do you ever think of Mandy? Do you ever think of me? Do you ever think of anyone but yourself? Isn't it time you got a little more responsible? Just a little bit." She is holding her hand up and pinching her fingers together. Then she straightens up and tosses her head back.

She looks sideways and sees him withdrawing into himself. This makes her even more furious. He always does this, she thinks. Just when I want him to talk to me, he won't. Fine. The hell with him. And she sits looking straight ahead, her eyes drilling into the darkness.

They drive silently for a while. He has seen that look before and it makes him uneasy. She seems a stranger to him and he doesn't know how to talk to her. He wants to turn her back into that bubbly loving person he fell in love with, but doesn't know how. This makes him feel frustrated and quite lost, rather like a little boy who has lost his mother in a supermarket.

He also realizes she has a point. He knows how she feels about heights, but ignored her feelings in his excitement in the mountains. As his shame grows, he becomes angry.

"Look, it wasn't my fault the damn road was blocked."

She continues to look straight ahead. "It wouldn't have hurt us to stay the night. Then we could have driven out tomorrow. Why was it so bloody important to risk our lives romping through the mountains like that? I've had enough of this. The sooner we get home, the better. I've never felt good about this trip anyway."

Jim says nothing. He is depressed thinking about how this trip is going so wrong. He has wanted to visit Provence for as long as he can remember. And he has even had thoughts about staying for a year or two, perhaps when he retires or takes a sabbatical. But he knows that Debbie will be reluctant because she doesn't like to go away from home for long. As they drive along glumly, Jim knows his dreams might be shattered by this trip.

After a couple of hours, they come to a small inn and pull up at the front gate. Jim enters the lobby and asks a portly balding man behind the desk "Avez vous un chambre pour ma femme et moi?"

The man looks up over his bifocals and says in slow, punctuated French "And what language do you speak, young man?"

"Uh, English."

The innkeeper, switching to English, says "I thought you might be German."

"No, I'm Canadian."

"Oh, you have come a long way."

"Yes and we are looking for a nice room. My wife and I have had a hard day. We got trapped in the mountains, and had trouble finding our way out. My wife is very upset."

The innkeeper looks sympathetically at Jim and smiles. "I'm Jacques," he says. "Bring your wife in."

The inn has lots of available rooms. Jim goes back out to the car where the cannons are still smouldering, but no longer firing. He smiles at her as he pulls their bags out of the car. She follows him silently up the stairs and into the inn.

They are given a large room overlooking a lake with mountains in the background. Jim opens a bottle of white wine they had brought with them and fills two glasses. Debbie sits on a sofa by the window and takes a sip, looks out to the mountains and then closes the shutters.

Jacques had insisted they go to the dining room for dinner, saying he would personally prepare something special for them. When they go downstairs, Jacques' three children are playing quietly on the dining room floor and his wife is tidying up the tables. There is one other couple sitting at the far end of the large room.

They sit down in the quiet, dimly-lit room with a candle on the table between them and begin to relax. Jacques comes over with a long stem red rose and presents it to Debbie. "For the lady who had a bad day," he said. "May her other days in France be filled with happiness."

When it is time to order the wine, Jim makes a selection. Jacques says "No, no, you don't want that one. It's a very good wine, but we can do much better than that for the same price.

He goes down to the wine cellar and returns in a few moments with a dusty old bottle of 1968 Chateau Neuf-de-Pape. After he displays the bottle and then twists out the cork, Jim takes a small mouthful and swirls it in his mouth, trying to sense all the subtleties of the smooth dry wine. Jacques smiles "Don't be too critical young man, or I'll drink it myself." They all laugh merrily.

The rest of the evening is spent with a delicious chateaubriand, the superb wine and a charming and attentive Jacques. After they finally return to their room arm in arm, they make love on the sofa by the window with the shutters open and the moonlight shining on the lake.

In the morning, Jacques is at the desk when they check out. After they pay the bill, he asks them to wait for a moment. Then he disappears downstairs and returns shortly with a bottle of Luberon wine. He says "This is a gift from me to you. When you are far away in Canada, drink this wine and send a thought my way." Debbie kisses him on the cheek and says "We'll send many thoughts your way, you can be sure of that."

Then they head out towards Avignon. "We have to get there before the sun goes down", says Jim. "Don't push your luck", she replies wryly.

It is a long drive, and they stop many times, so it is late in the afternoon when they buy some hot dogs and Perrier at a roadside stand. They decide to drive a little further and then stop the car beside the highway to eat. It is still a couple of hours to Avignon, but the road is good.

As they sit in the car, finishing their hot dogs and watching the sun go down, Jim says "There, two sunsets and nothing bad has happened."

"She smiles "Just no more mountains for a while, OK?"

"I promise", he says, rubbing her shoulder.

As he speaks, he notices a small black car entering the parking area behind them. The car is dirty and the windows seem smoky, but he can pick out two or three heads inside. As the sinister looking car slides to a stop, a tall young man jumps out and runs to the bushes with his hands unzipping his fly. Although they can still see the fading sunset, a light drizzle is starting, and a night chill is creeping into the car.

Jim wants to go and reaches to turn the key, but Debbie says "Just a minute" and opens the door. She stands beside the car and brushes the bread crumbs off her dress. Then she gets back into the car, but before she has time to close the door, the tall young man is suddenly leaning his head into the car. "Is Avignon this way?" he asks, pointing down the road. Jim glances down the road and says "Yes, I believe so".

When he looks ahead, he notices the dirty little car has driven in front of them and now sits with the side door open, but he doesn't have time to fully comprehend what is happening. As soon as he takes his eyes off the stranger, the tall young man reaches quickly into the car and grabs Debbie's purse laying in front of her legs. Before either of them can move, he is running towards the open door of the car in front.

Debbie screams "He's got my purse!"

Yesterday's images of her fear and anger flashes through his mind. It has all been so much better today. Yesterday his dreams seemed to be dying. Today they seem so much more possible. We can't have another bad day, he thinks, we just can't. And he jumps from the car and races after the thief.

Jim tackles the thief just before they reach the waiting car. Then he takes a couple of swings at the young man and they fall to the ground in a fierce struggle. Jim doesn't see the knife until it is too late. It rips across his chest and he falls back. Two other men are out of the car by now, and they jump on top of him with their knives flashing in the red glow of the sunset. Then they scramble into the car, the tires squealing onto the highway, leaving their victim lying in a large pool of dark red blood.

Debbie sits frozen in her seat and dimly sees the body lying on the ground. She absently picks up the long stem rose lying on the dash board and turns it in her hand and soon the crushed petals are strewn all over her dress. She begins to hum a tune, very quietly, as she looks straight ahead. The lights of the cars flash by on the highway as the sun goes down and the rain beats sorrowful rhythms on the hood of the little blue car.

HUNTER ON THE HILL

Abe and his son, Kale, sat in the front seat of the Cherokee and watched the sun breaking above the horizon with a red-orange glow that reflected in the frost of the fields. "It's beautiful," they kept saying. "Just beautiful." The words echoed in Abe's head with the hum of the tires on the road and the drumming of his fingers on the steering wheel.

After a long silence, Kale said, "You haven't taken me hunting for years."

Abe continued staring at the road, "Nope."

"Well, you and mom work a lot. Anyway, this reminds me of when grandpa used to take me to his old fishing camp. I learned to fish trout there. We would walk around behind the cabin and then down the path to the stream. It was real steep and rocky and it was hard to go down the path without falling. When I was little, I used to grab the tree branches. There was good fishing there."

"Not any more. Now it's all cottages and people. The stream is polluted. The people who bought the camp tore it down and built a prefab. They even have electricity and telephones out there now."

"It was nice while it lasted."

It was nice while it lasted, thought Abe. Yes, but we don't always have to accept what the world throws at us. We can change things, if we want to badly enough. Yes, he thought, it's time for a change. We will hunt far into the wilderness. We will go where no-one else goes. I know just the place.

His hands were sweaty on the steering wheel and he took a deep breath. He smiled to himself at the reaction to his suggestion that they get up at 4:30 AM to go deer hunting. "You're kidding. Get real! Nobody gets up that early!"

But when the time came, Abe walked into Kale's room and pulled the blankets away and said it was time and a grumbling and groggy son staggered out of bed. He was hung over, but Abe knew he would be and took some pleasure in rousing him out of bed.

As they drove, the fields yielded to thick forests which were glorious in their autumn colors mixed with pine and spruce trees. The highway had become a narrow unpaved road. They could smell the pungent air of the foothills and their heads were clear, even Kale's. It was fifty miles into the country and a half empty thermos of coffee lay on the seat between them.

"Why do we have to go so far into the woods? There must be deer along here."

"Better hunting farther in," said Abe. "Here they are hunted too much and know enough to stay away from people."

"We'll soon be in the high country. There are grizzlies and cougar there," said Kale, looking closely into the bush along the road.

"I came here for years. Never even heard of an attack around here. Don't worry."

The road grew narrower and rougher and it was a long time since they had seen any houses when finally they pulled into a small logging road and stopped. Both of them jumped out and stood beside the jeep facing the woods with steam rising up from the little yellow puddles spreading in front of them on the morning frost.

They pulled the rifles out of the back of the jeep, drew them from their cases and leaned them against the fender. Then, they put on the bright orange hunting vests. Kale picked up the old Winchester 30-30. It was a good bush gun with lever action, short and easy to handle in the woods. Abe took the 30-06, a longer and heavier bolt action rifle, with greater range. As Abe clipped on his 'scope, Kale got out the ammunition and put a handful of 30-30 shells into his pocket. Then Abe filled a clip with eight long copper-tipped bullets and dropped some extras in his pocket.

"There, that should be enough."

"Really," said Kale, "we're not going out to start a war."

Abe watched his son's stride as they moved silently through the forest. It was the straight-legged and confident movement of a strong young man. Not quite a swagger, but still revealing a chip on the shoulder. He had the wide shoulders and thick muscular body of his father.

It was this chip on the shoulder that first got the young man into trouble. It started with frequent fighting at school which led to slugging a teacher and a lengthy suspension. And then came the booze and drugs. Abe had stopped trying to figure out what had caused it all. It exhausted him to think about it and he knew he couldn't take much more.

He couldn't handle the young man physically anymore. That was proven a few months ago when Kale came home at breakfast time drunk and high and demanding the car keys.

When Abe grabbed Kale by the sleeve and told him to sleep it off, Kale landed a heavy fist on the side of his head and the next thing he remembered was Joyce leaning over him crying and holding his throbbing head in her arms. By then, Kale had gone out again and didn't come back for three days.

People at the next support group session, a group called "Tough-love", shook their heads sympathetically and a white-haired banker said they should do what he did when his eighteen year old decked him and pack the youngster's bag and put it outside the door for him when he came home.

"He'll get the message", said the banker.

Later, Joyce said none of this was the answer. "A family can't survive without love", she said as they pulled into the driveway. "Without love, there is nothing."

Joyce would never give up trying. Abe knew that, but he also knew it was destroying her. When he came home late from work one night about a year ago, he found her huddled in the corner of the basement behind the furnace with all the lights out. It was three months before she could function again.

For a while, everything seemed better, but then the troubles with Kale resumed. They noticed alcohol on his breath in the mornings and a couple of times they had to clean the stairs of vomit and wash all his clothes out. Later, the support group told them the kid should have done the cleaning himself.

Then they started noticing shortages of money around the house, like the money on the shelf in the bedroom that disappeared. This phase came to a head when Joyce realized that two of her favourite rings were missing. When they confronted him, he walked out for a week and then showed up one night dirty, hungry and hung over. They extracted many promises from him but the truce only lasted a couple of days.

Abe's glum thoughts lightened slightly as they walked through the forest dripping melted frost from the growing warmth of the sun. Red, orange and golden leaves lay on the ground but there was still lots of color on the trees. Rays of bright sunlight gleamed through the branches and they could hear the soft crunching of the leaves under their feet as they tried to walk as quietly as possible. The birds were starting to sing and once in a while a chipmunk would chatter at them from someplace high in the trees as they picked their way along the old trail. Kale peered intently among the trees and bushes.

This was a place where Abe had hunted as a young man with his father before he went off to law school in New York. He had met Joyce there, a transplant from Toronto in the advertising business, and after he graduated they were married. They didn't want to have children then but Kale arrived anyway and they found a day care center for him near Madison Avenue.

Abe knew the trail they were on very well. He knew it followed the contours of the hills, plunging through the deep forest and then into a wide open valley split in the middle by a rocky, sparkling steam. The area hadn't changed much and Abe could remember this place as though it were home. In the summer the trout fishing was always good and in hunting season, game could often be found by the stream.

On the south side of the valley, it was possible to walk through boulder strewn clearings all the way up to the rim of the valley. At the highest point, he and his father would sit on the rocks for hours looking across the forested hills and watching for deer coming to drink in the stream at sunset.

They would both have telescopic sights on their long rifles, but still it took a good shot to bring down a deer from that distance. Abe was the better shot and any time a deer appeared on the move, his father let him take it. In all their years of hunting together, he had never missed.

Kale stopped in front of him when they came to a clearing in the forest where the trail branched into two directions. Abe said they should split up. Kale would take the main trail along the stream which would come out of the forest on the valley floor and Abe would follow the smaller trail which would lead to the upper edge of the valley. If he saw a deer, he might be able to scare it down towards the forest on the other side of the stream, right past his son's gun-sights. He would fire a shot to let Kale know a deer was coming unless he thought it better to take the deer himself.

Abe walked fast after Kale disappeared into the trees beside the stream and soon was puffing up the side of the valley amid the rocks. He would sit by the rocks and wait for Kale to emerge from the trees into the open valley by the stream. He would be able to see him clearly as he made his way along the rocks by the stream.

The latest event had been the worst one. Kale came home high on crack and Abe took him to the hospital and they admitted him to the psychiatric ward for a month. When Abe and Joyce went to visit, Kale kept mumbling about wanting to die - that life wasn't worth living. Joyce collapsed and had to be admitted as well. Afterwards, she went back to regular therapy sessions, but she would often wake up in the night crying. When he moved to comfort her, he could see that he was losing her. When Kale got out of the hospital, they talked him into going with them back to Alberta for a month. Abe's sister still lived in the old house they had grown up in.

He sat by a large rock between some trees that shielded him from view and rested his rifle on the rock. He could see the whole valley. He drew back the bolt on his rifle and saw a copper-tipped cartridge spring slightly upwards. He slowly pushed the bolt forward and watched the cartridge slide into the firing chamber. Then he clicked the handle of the bolt down and firmly into place. For a while, he watched the point where the stream emerged from the woods but there was no movement. He lay his head against the rock and felt the soothing warmth of the sun.

After some time - he lost track of the time - there was a movement in the bushes and then he saw Kale striding along the edge of the stream into the clearing. The young man sat down on a boulder and rubbed his face with a handkerchief. Then he looked all along the floor of the valley and up along the ridge at the valley's edge. His gaze swept without hesitating past the spot where Abe crouched behind the boulder.

Kale began to walk gently and slowly along the edge of the trees into the valley. He stopped sometimes and looked all around and then resumed his slow trek. After about ten minutes, he stopped and sat on a log by the stream and stared into the rippling water.

All the while Abe watched from his distant and lofty perch. Once he raised the gun and watched through the scope, the safety on and his finger off the trigger but still feeling uneasy about breaking all the rules. Kale's hair had curled even more around his neck from the sweat. His back and shoulders looked muscular and powerful.

The next time he looked over the top of the rock, Kale was up again slowly moving along the stream. Every few steps, he stopped and listened and then moved on.

Many a time, Abe had dropped a deer running along that stream. He raised the rifle and watched through the scope and saw the side of Kale's head. He was surprised to see a smile grow on his son's face as he stopped moving and stared straight ahead.

Abe scanned the scope along the edge of the woods in front of Kale. He stopped when the circle of the scope showed a medium sized doe standing in a small clearing. The doe was frozen as still as a statue and looking directly at Kale. Both stood that way for what seemed an interminable length of time.

Kale had only to slowly raise his rifle and it would be an easy shot. But he just stood still and unmoving. Abe put down his rifle and watched the two of them and waited and slowly, ever so slowly, Kale was bending over. Then Abe watched in astonishment as Kale slowly picked up a rock and tossed it lightly at the deer. At this movement, the doe bolted and disappeared into the woods.

Abe stood up and fired his rifle into the air. When Kale looked up, Abe waved and then began to make his way down the hill to where his son waited. With all the rocks and the steep incline and the stream's slippery stones, it took about half an hour. All the while, Kale waited and smiled once in a while and listened to the woods.

When Abe was close enough, he said "Why in hell didn't you shoot?"

"Dad, he was so beautiful. His big brown eyes were looking straight at me."

Abe walked up to Kale and hugged him tightly. "Didn't know you were such a wimp."

"Jeez, Dad," said Kale.

Abe looked up at the sky. "We have lots of time to try for some trout. Let's go get the poles from the jeep."

THE PROJECT

Many places in the world have an odor that is unique to them and instantly sensed when you are there. One of the most beautiful is in southern Spain where the orange blossoms permeate the air like a sweet, fruity nectar. Or there is the pungent pine odor of the great forests of North America, stretching from the rich, dark soil in the heart of the continent, to the cold, hard rock of the ancient Canadian shield. And there is the damp floral fragrance of the Caribbean islands, always refreshed by the westward flow of the trade winds over the warm seas.

The subcontinent of India smells of masses of people. It's not a bad smell, and is as much of a feeling as a smell. It seems to make you aware that you are in the midst of one of the great congregations of humanity. And perhaps nowhere is the smell of humanity more powerful than in the streets of Calcutta, where fifteen million people are gathered to live out the trials of life in what can be the sorriest state of humanity. Here, there is suffering of a timeless intensity. Here we see an old beggar lying near death on the street and the crowds passing by on their daily movements, not because of insensitivity, but because they know there is nothing they can do and that there are so many others.

A tram stops to let off some passengers. It is rush hour and the tram is loaded as only a train in India can be, with people hanging from doors, and windows filled with a sea of faces. Faces looking absently past the old man and others looking blankly at him. Faces staring curiously and others looking with disgust. The old beggar is wrapped in the rags that used to be a loose, white robe and is lying on the side of the road on his back with his head slightly lifted as if to appeal but without the strength to do so. His lips are swollen and cracked and his face is gaunt and streaked with the hopelessness of pending death.

He is vaguely aware of the smell around him for this particular sense it is still quite strong. He is used to the smell for he has known it for all his forty years. He does not know it is forty years, and others might guess him as much as twice that unless they knew the ages of the beggars of the streets of Calcutta, or indeed, of the world. Today, the odor is accented by the sewage running a few feet from him in the gutters by the road. He is used to that as well.

He is also aware of the sounds, as his sense of hearing is particularly acute at his stage of existence. He can hear the wheels of the tram squealing on the tracks and the tramp of the feet near his head. He can hear the rumble of the wooden wheels on the stone road. He can even hear the sound of voices coming near and then fading away. Coming and fading. Not staying nearby for very long.

When he opens his eyes and strains hard, he can see as if in a thick mist. The shapes are mostly hazy but sometimes one comes close enough in his range of vision that he can make out some of the details. Mostly, however, he does not try very hard, and his eyes are closed, or only partly open and taking in very little.

His mind is befuddled, and the thinking process has largely stopped. He senses his surroundings but there is little reaction. Sometimes he sees strange shapes and lights but he does not know if they are real or not, whether he is dreaming or not. Reality and unreality are blending in the way that only those near death can know. He gasps for water, but no one hears and he lay his head on the dry cracked pavement and remains still and silent for a while. Some of the passersby assume that he has died and pass at a greater distance.

There are times when time seems not to move, but move it does, and sometime later the old man feels a drop of moisture on his face and when his feeble lids part, he is gazing up into the face of a craggy old woman who is bent over him and cradling his head in her arms. Her eyes reflect a sad compassionate wisdom, as she holds in the palm of her hand some water she has scooped from somewhere. He sees her through the same haze, which has thickened, but he can make out a thin white hood around her head as she leans closer and gently presses her lips against his forehead. He shrinks back at this unfamiliar gesture, but more in his mind than in his body, since his body is no longer responding to his will. Amid a delicate scent of lavender, his fading ears pick up the quiet words of the craggy old woman: "Be With God."

There is a sense of movement and a moment of confusion, as he cannot tell if he is moving or if it is his surroundings, which have changed to a liquid sort of rotation. Then there is a profound relief and calm as he gives himself to the movement, a kind of slow rhythm like a muffled drum, distant and pervasive and serene. Sometimes there are small points of light circling around him, which appear and then disappear like specs of dust floating in a beam of light. There is light coming from somewhere.

The surroundings solidify and he is sitting on an ornate carpet on a marble floor surrounded by great columns that seem to rise up out of sight. He also sees the structure from outside, as well as from where he is sitting and recognizes it as the same as a palace he once passed by and gazed at for a long time, until an occupant ran out and chased him away with a big stick that left bruises on his back and legs for many weeks. A tall man with a dark clipped beard is moving across the carpet towards him from a portal and stands before him.

"Welcome back, Lezsiha. You must now try to forget. There is little to reveal from examination. It is for the others to learn. You may now restore and resume your place when you are ready."

The confusion returns, as Lezsiha stares into the dark eyes of the tall man, which are calm and confident, peaceful and loving. He feels the hardness of the marble beneath his legs. He places his hands flat on the floor and pushes. He pushes as hard as he can. When he looks up, the tall man is gone. He rises effortlessly and walks lightly to the outside, where instead of sordid streets there is green countryside and flowing brooks and grassy meadows. The air is sweet and cool and scented with wild flowers. He sees a distant meadow beside which there is a large tree with wide swaying palm fronds. Suddenly he is standing under the tree and he lies down.

There was a time before this time when there was life. Then there was time but now there is no meaning in time.

That which is to be is in the past. I must know the past. He closes his eyes and lets the singing breeze in the palm fronds carry him on the wings of thought. He can still hear and feel the muffled drum.

There is a city street and he is walking in a bowler hat and dark striped suit. Carriages and hooves clatter on the cobblestones. He enters the law courts through a small wooden side door beside a pub on the corner and descends the narrow stairs and shuffles through dark corridors to a small office. He stands before a high sloped desk and with both hands pulls a large ledger from a shelf under the desk. He draws to his side a square box piled high with papers and begins to write in the ledger with one of the long quills standing in a pot. Aside from a half hour in the pub for a pint and a loaf with spiced pork and pickles, he works continually until the streets outside are dark and then he makes his way to a small tenement house near the docks where he has dinner with three children and a chubby, pleasant looking woman. Lezsiha smiles.

He then hears the pounding of horses' hooves on hard dusty soil. There is the screaming of men with their fighting blood high and the higher pitched screams of the wounded and dying. There are muscular brown men swinging great sharp swords as far as the eye can see on the wide, flat plains. On a knoll, surrounded by the largest and fiercest fighters, is a giant dressed in the finest silks and golden armour and sitting astride a great white stallion. His sword is scrolled in gold and silver and is dripping with the blood of those few warriors who manage to break through his defenses. The warrior closest to the King is the strongest and fiercest fighter and there are many bodies strewn around him. He is wearing a blue tunic, all torn and blood stained.

"Lezsiha, my lord, they have sent me for you. Can you follow?"

Beneath the palm trees, Lezsiha opens his eyes and before him is the warrior in blue standing neat and tall and surrounded by a clear, blue glow.

As Lezsiha watches, the blue tunic blends with the glow of the aura until the aura is almost the only thing visible, and then the body returns to sight again. It fades back and forth and Lezsiha realizes that the soldier is still talking to him, only his mouth is not moving.

"Aisgahr", he says, "my true and faithful friend." He rises without standing and realizes that his own body is now a blue glow and it touches and blends with the glow of Aisgahr. He can feel the strong throbbing life force of his friend and they communicate through this contact. Together, they float higher until the meadow and the pillars are far below them and then are gone.

The two orbs of blue light drift together, swirling around each other and sometimes merging and splitting apart and blending together again. Lezsiha feels a familiar comfort and peace in the unions and they are no longer speaking but simply sharing thought pulses and feelings. Other orbs of light come near and circle around them and each other. There are reds and many whites and some other blues. They greet in the same way, by touching and merging and circling. From a great distance, all glow as a single light but up close the individual colors can be distinguished.

A single purple light, strong and clear, enters from somewhere and all the others gather around and circle slowly. Now they appear as brightly glowing points of light in a vastness not unlike the dark majesty of physical space, speckled with brightly glowing stars. Through a silent telepathic communication, the purple one, the teacher, welcomes Lezsiha.

"You have done well, Lezsiha. We have observed your experience and all have gained a greater understanding. We are grateful to you for this demonstration. We will now open the class for questions."

Lezsiha's consciousness is now clear. It glows more brightly with the renewed energy from this acknowledgement and focuses completely on the teacher and on the questions of the other students. Some of the others draw upon this energy to strengthen their understanding. Sometimes the teacher speaks and then they all listen closely because they know that the teacher speaks from a much more complete knowledge of the Source than they possess, having nearly completed the transition from finity to infinity.

Later, as the questions subside, Lezsiha looks back to a street in Calcutta and sees the worn body of a ragged beggar being moved from its place by the sewer, where his head had been gently laid on a flat stone by a little bowed figure in a white robe.

THE RHYTHM OF THE SEA

The ocean is clear beneath the waves and I can see the sharply defined grains of sand and the minnows scrambling from my sudden intrusion. A few tufts of tall green sea grass dance with the waves. I can feel myself catapulting forward in the water. There is a sensation of moving and then rushing and I look ahead and feel the water cool against my face. I cannot breathe, but have no fear nor pain, only a warm, comforting peace. I can taste the salt water in my mouth and throat. I have a sense of wonder at the green tunnel of water through which I am moving. I am one with the ocean, like the dolphins we sometimes see out in the Gulf on clear, sunny days.

And then I am sitting on the beach wrapped in a blanket and eating an ice cream. My mother's eyes are red and she is saying it was a close call. My father tells how he happened to look up at the right moment - how he ran into the surf, and with a few strong strokes, grabbed me by the legs and pulled me out. They keep talking about it and soon they are saying the same things over and over again so I tune out and sit eating my ice cream and gazing out over the waves rolling onto the beach. Every seventh wave is the biggest, they say. I count the waves and watch for the big ones forming far out in the water.

It's a complex rhythm. Most of the waves curl into the shallows and slide up the wet strip of sand along the water, except that sometimes the biggest waves move with such force they overwhelm the smaller ones. And then a more regular rhythm begins again and I wait for the next big wave to come. If only I could know when the next one is coming. If I knew the rhythm, maybe then I would understand. How do we know which will survive and which will not?

They built the small white cottage on the beach when they were young. We stayed there many summers. When I was very small we walked together in the surf along the beach in the evenings while the sun was low in the sky and a light breeze was drifting in from the water. His hands were large and comforting. That is my strongest memory of him.

We went to the cottage every summer and stayed until school started. Sometimes I would have friends come to stay overnight, and she would often have her sister for company. Sometimes, someone would say to her that she should get married again, but her answer was always the same. "Billy was the only one for me," she would say. I heard her say that for years.

People could see the war coming. He had told her he would enlist. She was proud of him and said that she would always wait for him. The day after Hitler's tanks entered Poland, he went to the enlistment office and within a month he was heading for the ship. I remember them standing by the open, front door of our house and a car waiting on the street. I saw them kiss and hold each other for a long time and then they saw me on the stairs and we all hugged together. At the time, I only vaguely under-stood the importance of it all. She stood there a long time after he had gone, before she closed the door.

A big calendar was hanging on the wall beside them. The calendar advertised "Old Chum" pipe tobacco and fea-tured a large picture of a round man smoking a pipe and talking to a young boy standing beside a horse. They were English, dressed in turn-of-the-century riding clothes. In the background were a barn and some fields with rail fences around them. The fields were pristine and rather cartoon-like. Below the picture was a tear-off sheaf of pages stapled to the heavier paper of the calendar, one for each month. A few days after he left, she rolled it up and took it to her room.

He had been gone for over two years when, some-where east of Newfoundland, his convoy was attacked by submarines. The lead corvette had just developed engine trouble and had to move back. His ship moved up to the front. The torpedoes struck within minutes, according to the reports, and the ship went down quickly. Some survi-vors of the explosions and fire ended up in the water and the other ships managed to rescue some of them, but he was not among them. Lost at sea, said the letter simply.

I didn't see the letter then. She told me about it one day when I came home and caught her crying at the kitchen table. She raised her head and wiped her eyes on her blue, white-frilled apron and tried to smile. Then I was in her arms and we hugged for a long time without saying anything and cried together. At the time, I thought I was very close to her. But now I know you can never know your parents.

Not really. They live too much before you are born. And then when you are young, you know only part of them. By the time you learn to look beyond yourself, you no longer have the time to catch up to where they have been.

In her later years, she liked to sit for hours on a chair placed on the grass in front of the cottage and watch the waves rolling to the beach and the gulls picking periwinkles off the rocks by the shore. Sometimes she would gaze far out to sea and at those times we knew that she was no longer with us.

As so often happens, the physical parting came later. On a bright sunny morning, she walked into the ocean. We were in the cottage and it was quite a while before we realized she was no longer in her chair. They found her four days later. But I understand. I know how wonderful it would have been.

Great sheets of rain are slicing into the parking lot as I drive the car into the space nearest the door. I pull my collar tight and my hat low and rush into the deluge towards the entrance. I am hurrying not only because of the rain but also because I don't have much time.

I reach the main door stumbling in the deep puddles, already quite soaked, and then go inside and reach for the key she had given me. I step inside the elevator, gasping for air, and go to the apartment.

Inside, there is the quiet, stuffy feel of rooms that have been closed up and unoccupied for some time. But there is still a familiar odor, consisting of the faint mixture of gentle perfume and scented soap she favored along with the unique blend of furniture, clothing, plants and other things that people seem to create for themselves. It brings to me a calm, familiar feeling. I almost expect to see her coming through the door from the living room, her face bright with happiness at my visit, her arms extended for a hug and a kiss on the cheek.

There are some dirty dishes in the sink and a half cup of cold coffee on the kitchen table with a small lipstick stain on the rim. I empty the cup into the drain and fill it with water and leave it to stand in the sink.

There is not much of value here. The clothes will go to the Salvation Army and the dishes to the cottage. The furniture is old but well made and we will find a place for some of it, perhaps at the cottage.

When I enter her bedroom, there is the old calendar on the wall, still showing the same date - August, 1939. It was years before I realized the significance of the date. That was after I learned in school about the German tanks clanking into Poland in September of 1939, touching off the war. I began to ask questions, most of which went un-answered. It sometimes takes a long time to understand those who are closest to us.

On the dresser is a picture of the cottage, as it was in the forties. I am the bony little kid standing beside her on the lawn. She is wearing a cotton dress that reaches to her ankles. She is slim and the breeze is brushing her loose, blonde hair over her cheek. She looks strong and healthy and very pretty and is smiling broadly for the camera.

I don't know who was holding the camera, but it must have been someone she loved very much to have drawn such a beautiful smile.

There is also a picture of him. He is standing on the steps of a castle in Britain wearing his Navy uniform, dark and pleasant looking with a well-trimmed beard highlighting his light blue eyes. His build is strong and stocky like his father and me.

The letter is in the top drawer, still in its original envelope, and as I pull it out, another letter written in her hand falls out, one that had never been mailed.

My Dear Bill, It has been so long. I can't wait until we meet again. We will have so much to talk about. Every night, I can imagine you lying in your bunk, and remembering our last kiss. And I can see you looking out across the rolling swells of the North Atlantic and knowing those same waters roll up that beach – our beach – it must seem so far away. I watched every day for two years when the mailman walked up the drive until finally he handed me the letter and the waiting was all over. I stood with the unopened letter in my hand and looked at the envelope and felt a pain growing in my stomach and pressing into my chest until I sat down on the floor in the hall and slowly opened it.

Sometimes I think about that night when the torpedo struck. How it must have been. How the panic spread among men who had been jarred from their sleep and roused too fast from their bunks. How you ran to the side rail for the life boats but the ship sank too fast for them to drop the boats into the water and you found yourself in the water. And the water was so cold you lost your strength quickly and soon you were sliding into the dark green depths and couldn't understand why you didn't struggle. Why you had no desire to struggle. I hope that's how it was.

There have been so many long nights alone in bed waiting and wondering and trying to keep the terror and fears from my mind. Looking at the calendar on the wall by the bed and wondering what lay under that sheet for August, 1939. Wanting sometimes to tear it off but knowing it would end something I couldn't bear to end. Wanting at least to peek underneath and sometimes in silent moments alone slowly turning up the sheets of those unknown lost months I have lived without you and seeing only unused calendar pages, empty and unmarked and revealing nothing.

I want to tell you how it has been with Davy growing up. How proud I am and how much I love him and how much I miss you being a part of our lives. Maybe you know. Maybe you're watching and waiting.

I could not love you any more than I do.

I reach up to the calendar and carefully lift out the sheet for August, 1939. Then I gently pull it away from the staples that bind it to the calendar. I fold it and place it in the envelope with the letter. There will be a moment when we will be left alone, and I will give her one last gift to close another door.

LOVE IN THE SHADOWS SOFTLY WAITS

A quick kiss. The quiet words "I love you" floating softly in the gentle midsummer breeze. A hastily opened window. A rush behind the rose bush and through the hedge. A father enters the front door. A girl shares her secret with the full moon. Smiling and smiling back.

The telephone rings. "I'll get it in the study," I say.

The mature but timid female voice speaks my name. It seems as though the voice should be familiar.

"Yes, this is Frank."

"It's Susan."

Nothing.

"Susan Gillien."

"My God, Susie. Is it you? It's - it's been twenty-five years."

"How've you been, Frank?"

"Oh well, busy, you know. Wife, four kids, job. All that stuff."

"They must be big, now."

"Yeah, three in university, here in Calgary, They're all living at home. Too good to them, I guess."

"You married Arlene Francis. I knew you would."

"Yes. I was sorry to hear about Derrek last year. A heart attack?"

"It came out of nowhere. There was no warning. He just died out in the driveway one morning. I found him in the snow when I was leaving for work."

"Where are you now? Still in Toronto?"

A tired edge enters her voice. "I'm in Edmonton now."

"Back in Edmonton? So close? Wow."

"Putting your life back together can be a tough," she says. "I'd thought I'd do it on familiar territory."

Then she says more brightly. "I'm sorry. Perhaps I shouldn't have called. I just wanted to see how you were. Perhaps when you're up this way, we could have lunch together. I'm working for IBM. In consulting."

I lower my voice. "I don't get up there very often. But sure. Perhaps. I'll call."

She interjects quickly. "Do you ever see Jack? Have you kept in touch with him?"

"Believe it or not, he's still my best friend."

"I thought likely. How is Dr Kingsley? Is he still at UCLA?"

"Oh, you know Jack. Same old guy. Such a strong personality doesn't really change much."

"I've talked to him a couple of times. And I've read about him in the papers," she says.

"Did you know there's a serious movement to nominate him for a Nobel prize? For his work with DNA," I add.

"Yes. Imagine. Our Jackie, the rink rat," she continues. "I heard he married a model from L.A."

"That was the last one. No. Now he's married to a young actress."

"My goodness, that must be number four."

"Five. Maybe he'll get this one right."

We talk for a few minutes and then I can hear Arlene finishing the dishes. Walking towards the study.

I interrupt the conversation. "I'll call. When I'm in Edmonton. I can get you through IBM?"

"Yes. Uh. Yes. Just call the switchboard. Ask for Susan Gates."

"Gates. Of course. I almost forgot. I'll call."

Arlene pokes her head in the door just as I hang up.

"A business call," I say.

"That was a neat way to get out of drying the dishes." She smiled. "Do you and your partners have a pact?"

"Just a moment. I have a couple of calls to make."

"Yeah right." A hug. A kiss on the cheek. "Let's go watch the movie."

I can't concentrate on the movie. The next day, I can't even recall which movie it was or who was in it.

Two weeks later, in mid September, I am in Los Angeles on business. I dial the university.

"I'm sorry. Dr Kingsley is tied up."

"You better call the police."

Irritation enters the voice. "I'm sorry?"

"Tell him it's Frank."

She replies in a huffy tone. "One moment please."

The boisterous good-natured voice comes on the line. "Frank, when in hell are you going to stop pissing off Marie?"

"You'd think she'd recognize my voice by now."

"None to bright, kid. None too bright. But she adds to the decor."

"Yes, I understand, Jack." I say this with a little friendly sarcasm.

Big laugh. I always liked Jack's big laugh. Always the laugh of a guy who has the world by the tail. Even in his rink rat days he laughed like that. "Hopefully," he says.

"I got a call from Susie a while ago."

"Susie? Not Susie Gillien."

"Yeah."

"Son of a bitch. How's the old girl doin'? I talked to her about six months ago. I was in Toronto. Seems she read in the Star I was there. Called me at the hotel. We had a nice chat. I was tempted to ask her over, but she had just lost Derrek. It was too soon."

"Too bad about Derrek. It was unexpected, I guess."

That big laugh again. "Probably fucked himself to death."

"Jesus, Jack." But he's like a brother. I've known him since we were toddlers living next door to each other and playing cars in the sand.

"You free tonight?" I ask.

"Yeah. C'mon over to the house. I have a bottle of Courvoisier with our name on it. You can meet Lisette."

Back in Alberta, just before Christmas, we are visiting with Arlene's parents in Edmonton, trimming the tree. Arlene's mother is talking. I'm half listening. Then something she says brings me to alert. A name.

"Did you hear," she says to Arlene, "Did you hear that Susan Gillien died? I read it in the paper. We knew her family. She died at the end of October. At least that's when I read the obituary. I meant to mention it. I think Frank went to school with her, didn't he?"

"I didn't know her," says Arlene. But I remember the name. She went to our high school. Didn't she Frank?"

I am concentrating with all my might on hanging an ornament without dropping it. My heart is pounding. "Yes, I knew her well. I didn't know. I hadn't heard."

Arlene looks at me curiously.

"Her mother continues. It was cancer, they said. It was in her bones. One of the worse kinds. I suppose she came home to die."

"I heard she got a job with IBM here."

"She worked for them in Toronto. Seems they agreed to move her out here even though there wasn't a real need. A humanitarian gesture, they say." Arlene's mother is always so well plugged in.

And she isn't finished. "Whenever I think of Susan Gillien, I think of that Kingsley boy. I never liked that boy. I know he's smart. But he's sneaky. Sneaky as they come."

She continues without a break. "He left that poor girl. Everyone knows what he did. And then when the baby was born - they say it was badly retarded - it ended up in some home down in the states, in Chicago, they say. You would have thought he'd show more responsibility. Leaving that poor girl like that."

"Jack is my friend," I say.

In the car on the highway back to Calgary, Arlene asks "You seemed shocked. Had you kept in touch with her?"

"She called a while back. Right out of the blue. She didn't say she was dying. She seemed to want to talk."

"Did you?"

"Yeah, for a while."

"You didn't mention it."

"I didn't know what to think. I thought she might be on the rebound. I didn't know."

"Well, It's good you talked to her," says Arlene, lying back in her seat. "You knew her well? How well? You've never mentioned her."

"Oh, I went with her for a couple of months before you and I met, after Jack dumped her."

Arlene opens her eyes with a scowl. Then says sarcastically, "Poor dear, sweet Jack. He'd never do such a thing. The S.O.B."

"He's always been a good friend to me."

"That's what you always say. But I love you anyway." She lays her head back again. Then mumbles, "Always thought he made a good rink rat. I didn't know you were into his left-overs."

"That was the only time," I say.

In the darkness, she doesn't notice my mood shifting - a depression settling in. Memories riding along between us on the dark Alberta highway.

The rink was an outdoor one. There was an old shack behind it, away from the road, maintained by a community association. Inside there was an old wood stove and benches for people to sit on while they changed their skates. The shack always smelled of wood smoke, wet clothes and hot chocolate that Jack brought in from his house around the corner.

Jack was in charge, appointed by his neighbour who chaired the rink association. The job involved opening the shack at certain hours, stoking up the wood fire and generally maintaining the ice and making sure the skaters didn't get hurt. The pay was small, but not insignificant to a young student. Jack had many friends and sometimes cut them in when they helped.

On Saturday nights, the young people - Jack's friends mostly - gathered and hung out. I used to go. Susie went and so did many others, including Mac, who was a big affable intelligent guy always into a new fad. Now he's a lawyer. At the time, he was hurting from recently being jilted by Carla Jamieson, a black-haired beauty from a nearby community,

For a while, Mac was practicing hypnotism. He practiced on his friends, if they let him. Mac was good at the hypnotism. But some people made better subjects than others. Mac always said the higher a person's intelligence, the faster they would go under. Naturally, everyone was eager to see him try it on Jack. But Jack always refused until that fall Saturday night when the shack had recently been opened for the new season and he had a couple of beers out back.

The shack was full and vibrant with anticipation. Jack sat on a stool by the stove and Mac stood in front of him, slowly swinging the watch. His soothing voice was saying things like "You are relaxing." You are getting drowsy." You are going to sleep." Suzie stood just behind and to the right of Mac, watching and listening intently and I was standing beside her.

Sure enough, Jack was the fastest of the group to go under. And he was in deep. We all had seen enough of them by then to know that. Mac asked him the usual array of little introductory questions. But it didn't take him long to close in for the kill.

"How much do you love Susie?" The answer came back unhesitatingly, "I don't know."

"Do you love her a lot?"

"Don't know. Good piece - uh - - -."

"You must love her?"

"Don't really like her guts."

"You what?"

"Her guts."

An odd answer. The subconscious trying to evade the truth. Susie was standing close enough that I could hear her jagged breathing. People were looking at her, trying not to stare. I could feel her nearness - warm and soft and vulnerable. I wanted to take her in my arms.

She said with a forced half-smile, "It's my guts."

Mac wasn't finished. Now his agenda was clear to some of us. But there was nothing we could do but watch.

"Who do you like better?"

"Don't know, lotsa girls."

"Like Carla? You like Carla, don't you?"

"Carla? Yeah.Carla." There was actually a leer on Jack's face.

Susie ran from the shack into the cold night. Concerned, I followed her and walked her home. I spent a long time talking to her.

A few months later, she left town for a year. Her family said she went to stay with her aunt. People were not fooled. This is the way these things were handled in those days. To escape the disgrace, they said. But she never even said good-bye.

A couple of days after we get back from Edmonton, I call Jack's office to wish him Happy New Year.

"I'm sorry, Dr Kingsley is out of town," says Marie.

"Oh, do you know how long he'll be?"

"He's in Chicago. A few days, he said."

"Chicago. Again. - - I suppose."

"It's a personal trip."

"I know. Tell him his friend called."

"Dr Kingsley has lots of friends. Could I give him a name?"

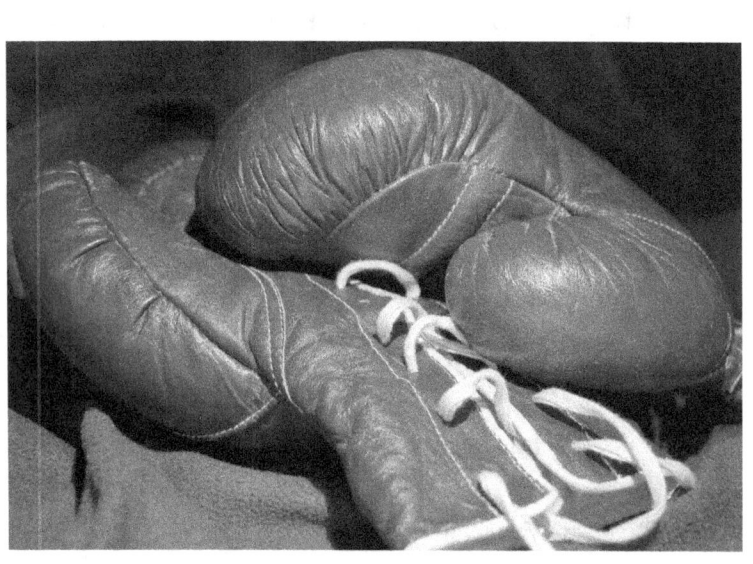

OF ROCKS AND HARD PLACES

Mark thought he would scream if the kid in the next block didn't stop crying. The ruckus had started at around two o'clock in the morning. Some kid was drunk and had been fighting at the Friday night dance in the Knights of Pythias hall. After beating up several other young men, he had busted out some windows and terrorized people on the street until the police came.

Two cops had managed to get him into the cruiser and down to the jail, but then he started yelling he had a right to make a telephone call. The police tried to get him into the drunk tank until he sobered up and settled down, but he wouldn't go. He grabbed the bars around the door of the cell and they couldn't pry him loose. When one of them punched him on the back, he whirled around with a wild swing and sent the tallest officer sprawling down the hallway.

The struggle lasted for ten or fifteen minutes. There were four policemen and when they finally went back to the front office after the fight, they were bruised and bleeding and their uniforms were torn.

The only reason they were able to get him into the cell was because his will to fight had suddenly died, and he had stepped inside and sat down. Then the tall cop had walked up and given him a couple of hard whacks on the head, mostly in revenge. Then they went out and locked the cell. He sat down in the cell and looked around him at the locked door, grungy cement floors, the black bars and the stained, dirty cot and he started to cry.

Mark lay in the next cell and waited for the commotion to quiet down. Then when it did, he still couldn't sleep. So he lay back on his cot and looked through the window-bars at the dark and starry sky. He thought about Linda and why she had done this to him. He kept thinking it wasn't going to help her or him. When the police had come for him, he was still recovering from his last fight. He looked like hell. Puffy eyes. Bruised face. Cut lips.

The fight had been intended as his first step into the big time. He had challenged MacKenzie, one of the top contenders for the National Championship. Mark had won on a TKO in the ninth round. However, some people had said that the victory wasn't decisive enough; that Mark had taken too many hard hits; that he wouldn't last very many years taking that kind of punishment.

Mark found that hard to accept. He began to make excuses, like the fact that his marriage with Linda was going on the rocks at the time, and he found it hard to concentrate on training. But deep down he knew they had a point. He had been surprised and a bit dismayed at how hard it had been to beat MacKenzie.

Linda and he had divorced during training, and she had won the right to alimony, despite the fact he didn't have a regular job. She said, as she had all along, that he should find one, that he was a skilled mechanic and there were jobs available. But he wanted to fight. Other than working a few years as a mechanic, fighting was all he had done. He loved the world of boxing. It's hopes and dreams. It's characters. The sweat and the grinding work. The moments of triumph when a tough opponent lay beaten in the ring and the referee held your hand high and the deafening cheers of the crowd drowned out the referee's words.

When he didn't make the alimony payments, she had taken it to family court, and they put him in jail for a week. His money for the fight would cover the backlog, but he hadn't yet received it. Now, he had a few more days before the week was up.

In the morning, they moved Roger out of the tank and into the cell next to Mark. There were just bars between them, and he watched Roger flop onto the cot. Surprisingly, Roger wasn't marked up very much from the fights, although he was dirty and his hands were scratched and bruised. He had black, curly mid-length hair and appeared to be a little over six feet tall, about eighteen and very well built. He looked like a weight trainer. He wore a tank-top and his shoulders and arms rippled with large well-proportioned muscles. Roger was clearly in shape, and no doubt very strong. Of course that was obvious from the previous night.

After a while, the police came in with breakfast. Roger, because he had been in the tank, was given a slice of dry bread and a cup of water. Mark was given bacon and eggs, toast and coffee. "Want some of my toast?", he asked.

Roger winced and said " No thanks" and groaned. He drank his water in one gulp. Mark said "How about some coffee? It'll make you feel better." Roger nodded, and Mark poured some of his coffee into the tin cup held against the bars.

They began to talk and Roger described how he had been raised in a small fishing village further north and his father had drowned at sea a few years before. His mother had remarried after a year, but Roger couldn't get along with his stepfather. When they got into a fist-fight one day, and Roger knocked out the two-hundred forty pound man with one quick jab, he had been told to find another place to live. His mother arranged for him to move into his uncle's basement, but he didn't stay there long. One day, he told them he was going to look for work along the coast and left town.

Since then he had been knocking around, following the lobster season as it opened in different sections of the coast hauling traps on the boats or else doing small jobs around the docks. He started drinking more often, and sometimes would go on real benders, in some cases lasting several days until he ran out of money for the bootleggers. During these bouts, he always turned wild, looking for fights and causing trouble.

As Roger drank the steaming coffee, he gradually began to come to life and his eyes ever took on some sparkle. Mark thought that here was a kid who under different circumstances might have done a lot better. He was surprisingly articulate and intelligent. When Mark told him that he was a boxer, Roger asked all kinds of questions and grew more animated and the two quickly began to form a bond.

An old fisherman Roger had been working for came in later that day to post bail and Roger was released. But before they said good-bye, Roger and Mark agreed to meet the following week to work out together at Al's Gym down by the harbour.

Al's Gym was in a renovated shed on an old repair dock. There was a row of windows overlooking the harbour so you could see the water and the boats going by while you worked out. In the center of the gym was a boxing ring and around it were punching bags, including speed bags and heavy bags and several old sets of weights, with benches, abdominal boards and squat racks. The floors were covered with ragged grey gym mats. Upstairs was a storage area which Mark had converted into a rough apartment, where he lived.

A few days later, they meet in the gym. Mark is standing in the corner of the ring in his dressing gown looking across to Roger, standing in the other corner. Roger keeps looking out the window at the harbour. He looks relaxed, even nonchalant. Mark feels tense. Roger's lack of concern bothers him. They drape their gowns over the ropes in their corners. Rogers muscled arms shine in the lights, pumped up because he has been working out all afternoon. They have decided to try some sparring before leaving the gym for the day.

Al, a balding ex-lightweight with a round red-veined bulbous nose, has agreed to be the referee and the two fighters move in to the center of the ring. They circle around each other and flick a few tentative, exploratory jabs. Roger moves easily and quickly for a big fellow.

But Mark is no slouch either and has several years of experience over the younger man.

After a few minutes, they are moving against each other more aggressively. Mark lands a solid blow to the body and sees that Roger feels it. Then Roger slips one in, right in the pit of the stomach. Mark feels his breath taken away and before he can recover, he sees a blur out of the corner of his eye. It is too late.

Mark experiences a drifting feeling and his eyes flicker open. He realizes he is looking up into Al's concerned face. Roger is standing by the edge of the ring, looking out at the harbour. He is calm and quiet. Mark doesn't know how long he has been out. He has never been knocked off his feet before. His first thought is that Roger's good. Really good. The fight had lasted less than a round.

Watching with rapt attention from a stool in a corner of the gym was Al's daughter, Lisette. She worked for Al cleaning the gym each day and keeping the books. She happened to be there when Roger came in and naturally wondered who was this good-looking lad with such a jaunty air of confidence. As she sat transfixed on her stool with a mop in her hand wearing faded jeans and an old red flannel shirt of her father's, her black hair tied back in a bun for work, Roger couldn't help but notice this very beautiful girl, who was almost exactly his age. As he looked out at the harbour, he was watching her from the corner of his eye.

Over a beer after the fight, Al said he never saw anything like it. "The old one-two", he said, bobbing back and forth. But so fast and so hard.

After that day, Roger and Mark met almost every day at the gym. They sparred together, but with helmets and heavy gloves. Once in a while one or the other would be knocked down, but neither was knocked out again.

Roger lifted weights a lot and moved some of the weight equipment around so he could watch the boats going out to sea as he worked. Sometimes, when he wasn't exercising, he would sit and watch them for hours. At such times he was very quiet, and the others in the gym almost forgot he was there. All except Lisette, who would some-times sit down beside him and look out over the harbour, not saying very much the first few days. He was very shy of girls and it took a few weeks before he talked openly with her.

Everyone else in the Gym knew you didn't get involved with Al's daughter, not only because you'd never get into the gym again, but because you'd have Mark to deal with. Mark was her self-appointed protector. Roger was una-ware of this, but anyway, Mark approved of the budding romance. Al seemed not to notice. All he talked about was how great things were going to be. The big time.

When Roger was sparring, everyone in the gym would watch. They would gather around the ring and when the going got rough, they would shout and cheer, just like at a real fight. After a few weeks, Roger had beat every chal-lenger in the gym. No one could touch him and he was their idol.

Besides being owner of the gym, Al was also Mark's trainer. Of course, Al began to give Roger tips on professional boxing, such as how to measure the skills of his opponent and pace himself accordingly. Roger learned quickly and showed keen interest in what Al had to say.

Al began to arrange fights for Roger with others in the community and nearby cities. Roger always won easily and his reputation as the one to beat was rapidly spreading. One day, after they were finished training for the day, and the three were talking, Al said" Why don't you go for the big time, Roger. You could do it."

Roger turned away from the window and said "Do you think so Al? I never thought about things like that. Well, you know, I never thought I could do it."

"I beat MacKenzie", said Mark, "and you can beat me".

"I feel good in the ring", said Roger. "It's like I'm in charge of something. I know how it's going to end. And when. And it always does."

"We'll help you get even better", said Al. "I'll be your coach and Mark will be your trainer. You'll go all the way. Right to the top. You'll see."

After that, the training intensified. Every day at the gym, the three men could be found lifting weights, working the heavy bags and speed bags, and sparring. They also went jogging along the coast road, with Al driving his car and Mark and Roger trailing behind. Roger moved in with Mark above the gym.

In the evenings, Roger and Lisette would be seen strolling along the beach and sometimes when the water was calm enough he would take her for a row in an old skiff left lying by the rocks near the gym. And they would talk as lovers always do.

"Do you truly love me?"

"Of course. You know I do."

"Mark says you used to be really wild."

"Used to. Now I want to win the title. Going all the way."

"I'm going with you."

People started to come to the gym from miles around to watch the fights, especially when someone from their community was coming over to spar with Roger. One of these visitors was a hood named Eric, who came in his old beat-up chevy with speed-balls hung around the windows and streamers on the radio antenna. Eric didn't box but was well known as a street fighter, who very few people messed with. When he came to the gym, he would lean against the wall near the door and hang his thumbs in his belt and sneer at the passersby.

Roger and Eric had met before. Eric would often go to a nearby dance hall and sit on the stairs at the entrance, waiting for someone to bump into him. When it was a young man, he would stand up and belt him. Usually the unfortunate victim didn't last long. Eric and Roger had always avoided each other in these encounters. Probably it would have been different if Roger had shown up on one of his binges while Eric was sitting on the stairs, but that hadn't happened yet.

Once in a while, after Eric had nailed several young fellows this way, someone would call the Mounties. One night when they came to take him in, he jumped on top of the cruiser and invited them to come and get him. When they came near, he kicked at them and kept them at bay for quite a while. A crowd gathered and he was having a great time showing off. Finally one of the Mounties pulled him down and a few of Eric's friends came to his assistance. The Mounties picked out some of the bystanders to help them control the situation and one of the "volunteers" was Roger.

Roger was cold sober that night and, like many of the bystanders was reluctant to get involved. However, he stood out in the crowd and when the Mountie pointed at him he waded in. Within thirty seconds, three of Eric's friends were lying unconscious beside the cruiser. Then with his blood up he headed for Eric, still struggling with one of the Mounties. Eric saw him coming and what had happened to his friends and got into the cruiser. On the way in, however, he said to Roger, "You're dead meat, man. Fuckin' dead." Roger shrugged and walked away.

Roger didn't see Eric much after that night, because it was only a few days later that he met Mark and started to spend all his free time at the gym. On the few occasions when Eric came to the gym, Roger didn't pay much attention to him.

This went on for about a year, while Roger beat all the local and regional contenders. Finally, they arranged a bout with MacKenzie and it took place on a hot, muggy June night in the Halifax Forum. They drove there on the day of the fight, to save costs.

MacKenzie has longish blonde hair and is bigger than Roger, with about ten pounds and two inches of reach over the younger man. But MacKenzie's age is beginning to catch up on him. Roger decides to go easy for a few rounds and try to tire his opponent and then close in around the fifth or sixth round.

Halifax is a fight city and the Forum is filled to capacity. The crowd has heard a lot about the brash young upstart and roars with delight when he enters the ring. Roger looks up at Mackenzie when the referee draws them together to shake hands, and his eyes are calm and cold. He lightly touches the other fighter's glove and abruptly turns to his corner, leaving MacKenzie standing alone for a moment. The moment seems to last for a long time.

When they come out, MacKenzie keeps Roger back with his superior reach and they toy with each other for the first round, with neither one scoring any real hits. Already at the end of the first round, the crowd is beginning to show some impatience. They expect blood. Then in the second round, Roger gets one of his short quick jabs into the body and MacKenzie steps back, surprised at the force. Roger begins to get more of them in and starts working on MacKenzie's body. MacKenzie can't seem to avoid the body blows, and by the end of the third round is slowing down badly and still hasn't really hit Roger.

In the fourth round, Roger starts going for the head. He connects one after the other, but MacKenzie's a tough fellow and keeps going. Roger starts to cut him and soon the blood is all over both of them. MacKenzie is being blinded by the cuts on the tissue around the eyes, soft and scarred from years of battering. The bell saves the fight from being called. But in the next round, Roger connects several hard cross hits to the head and MacKenzie is standing with his hands hanging at his sides. He is out on his feet and as the towel arcs over the ropes into the ring, MacKenzie crashes to the canvas and lies motionless. He is still unconscious when they carry him from the ring. Later in his dressing room, he is finally brought to consciousness, but his boxing career is over. He never did land a real punch.

The crowd goes wild and Roger is carried out to the dressing room on the shoulders of many new friends. Later in the evening, they drive back home. He and Lisette, Al and Mark all in Al's old Ford. Roger looks and feels superb and they go straight to a party at the gym.

Booze is not normally allowed in the gym, but this is a special night and almost everyone in the community is there. Roger hasn't been drinking during training, but he has a few beers and then switches to rye and ginger ale. After a while he climbs into the ring and offers to take on anyone there, one at a time, then two at a time, then three. There are no takers. But it spoils the mood of the party and people start to drift off. Eric is sitting at a table drinking rum and coke, and getting very drunk and leering at Lisette, who is sitting on her stool crying over Roger's behaviour.

Around midnight, most people have left and Roger is now quiet. It's been a long day and he makes his way out the door. Eric is slouched on the stairs with Lisette pinned against the wall beside him. She is struggling and he is pulling at her jacket. Roger cuffs him on the back of the head and yells at him to get away from her. Cursing, Eric pulls a four-inch switchblade from his pocket and lunges. Roger's fist catches him full in the face with such force that Eric is thrown backwards through a railing and lands on the rocks by the water.

Roger jumps down on the rocks and begins to pummel Eric with solid heavy blows. Quickly, Eric is lying still and Roger keeps slugging, the blows thumping sickeningly into the limp body. There is a dull snapping sound of ribs and other bones breaking. Lisette is screaming for Roger to stop, but he keeps on, a distorted visage of cold fury, such as she could never have imagined on this face that she loved - once loved - thought she loved - she didn't know. She turns and runs wildly up the hill to her father's home.

She cries into her father's chest and he holds her, rocks her. "He scares me", she says over and over. He says, "It's only when he's drinking. When he's not drinking, he's the best boxer I ever saw, everything I've ever dreamed of. Maybe we can stop him from drinking. We have to stop him."

Mark comes out the door just in time to see her leaving, to see how hurt she is. He jumps down and hauls Roger off Eric, whose breathing is raspy and gurgling.

"Roger, You're going to kill someone one of these days. I want you the hell out of here. Don't go near her again. If you hurt her, I'll kill you."

"You gonna make me - huh? C'mon, try it."

"I will if I have to." He pointed down to Eric, groaning on the rocks. "I know you can beat me, but you're going to have to do that to me too. And I can tell you I won't be as easy."

Roger springs forward. He raises his big rock-hard fists and feels the power of his tensing muscles. He sees the slight roll of flab above Mark's belt, which has survived the training. Mark surveys the curly headed youngster and this is the last thing he wants. But he assumes a boxer pose. Roger stands for a moment ready to strike, a coil-spring of power and danger. Then he suddenly relaxes and his eyes soften and he turns and walks up the stairs. In a moment, he returns with his kit-bag slung over his shoulder and without speaking walks down the road towards the highway. Mark stands there and watches and then he sees Lisette walk timidly down the hill from her place and fall into step beside him. He watches them until they are out of sight.

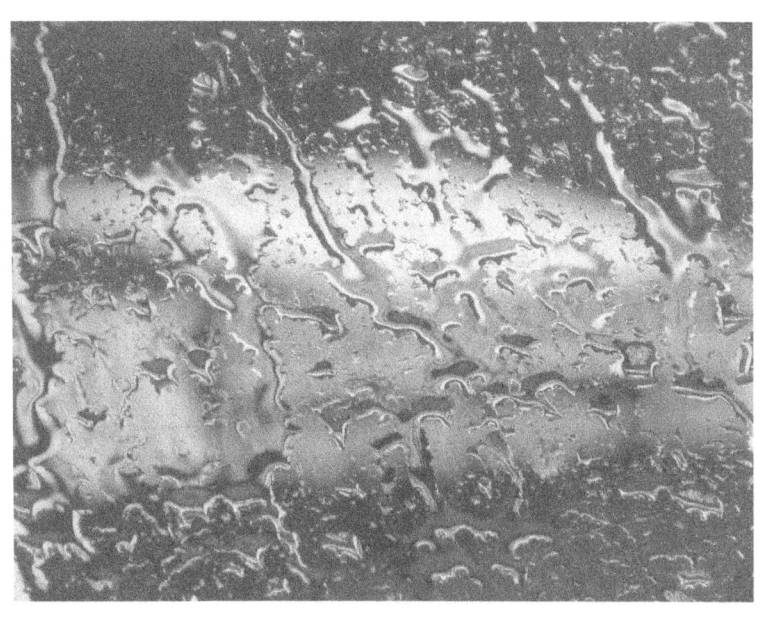

NIGHT OUT AT THE BRIGHT SPOT

Brody was sitting alone in a restaurant booth staring blankly through the wet, streaked windows to a parking lot that was mostly empty. The evening was grey and dismal like the day that came before it and the only color was the pale reflection in the rainwater of the last vestiges of a dull sunset glowing through a distant break in the clouds. There were two cars parked outside - the one he rented that morning and the one belonging to the owner of the restaurant. The rain was steady and relentless and cold. It was New Year's Eve.

His gaze was fixed out the window and Keats was his soulmate. "My heart aches and a drowsy numbness pains my sense." This was his motto, the theme of his life. He could see the young poet sitting under a tree beside a forest gazing morosely into the deep dark woods and he knew how his soul cried out to fly from his weak and tired body. He could feel his pain.

The restaurant in which he sat was a relic of the fifties. The Carrolls had been given it by Ed's mother, Ellen. It was a clean and well kept restaurant, nothing fancy, but the only place in town that still sold milk shakes made on the spot from fresh milk and ice cream and served in a big metal container straight from the mixer. And you could still get a good chocolate malted milk and fries made from freshly cut potatoes and hamburgers cooked with onions on a big flat grill that must have gone back the whole forty-odd years.

Ellen still liked to help out with the restaurant sometimes. She was a little white haired lady and such a bundle of energy that she made Brody tired just watching her. He could hear her talking as she bustled around wiping counters and sweeping floors. She often rattled on to anyone sitting in the restaurant. Sometimes it seemed as though it wouldn't matter if nobody was around.

People certainly liked her and the restaurant had built up a large and loyal following. Sometimes she waited on tables, even at eighty-two, with more energy than most of the teenagers they hired part-time. She was quite something. People often said she was why the restaurant was called "The Bright Spot".

The juke box was full of songs from the fifties and sixties. Brody could hear the sound of Elvis singing "Don't be Cruel". It was one of his first hits, way back then. Brody was thinking it was supposed to be a song to a lover, but maybe Elvis was really singing it to life. Maybe not at first, but later on. If he was, the plea was in vain.

Brody looked at Ed standing nearby wiping the counter with a damp cloth. Ed glanced at Ellen to make sure she was not looking and then smiled at Brody, and silently mouthed her words, "Charlie's coming. It's wonderful. Charlie's coming." For the past hour, she had been literally bouncing around the restaurant. Tidying up. Straightening out menus standing between paper napkin holders and salt and pepper shakers. Running to the window and looking out and running back again, and talking all the while.

"It was only a few months after I started this restaurant that I met Charlie and the boys. On New Year's Eve in 1929. I remember the date well because we were bringing in a new decade, not something we'd get to do very often. We were real excited about the thirties coming - - -. " She paused, then went on.

"But then the depression started soon after and then when that ended, the war started. We were young people but a lot of our dreams were destroyed one way or the other."

Brody heard himself say, "A lot of our dreams don't seem to work out."

Then Ellen stopped dead in her tracks and looked sharply at both him and Ed. "1935 it was when I got married and then five years later I was a war widow with two kids to feed. Don't talk to me about broken dreams." Then without a break she went back to her story. "The boys come in about a quarter to twelve and ordered some fish 'n chips and - - -."

Brody looked out the window again. He had heard the story a million times. Not that it was a bad story. It was kind of quaint, really. It went back to a time when people didn't move around so much, when they used to stay together for a whole lifetime. They would start out playing with the other kids that they went to school with and then married and did business with and went to chamber of commerce meetings with and then grew old with. Ellen's generation had a twist to deal with too. They went off to war and got killed together. It was a cruel twist, but they came out of it, those who did come out of it, with something special. A dignity that said they had learned something about life that others didn't know. Brody could see that dignity in her. He didn't understand it, though. He found the whole thing depressing.

The boys. The Pine Tree Gang. A piece of local folk-lore. That first night they came, Ellen had been hoping to sneak next door at midnight and sing Auld Lang Syne with everyone at the old Meeting House. Then afterwards she would rush back and put on lots of coffee for the people who stopped by on the way home. But when the boys came in, she was stuck because she had no one else to serve them.

They were fun for her though and she didn't really mind. They were all about her age -about twenty - and good looking boys, she said, and full of fun. They didn't drink or smoke and they went to church together. Hard to imagine. Brody had never known any gangs like that. More than likely they'd swarm you nowadays and take your money to buy some grass or coke. Times have sure changed.

In fact, they had just come from the church when they showed up at her restaurant that night. There were four of them and afterwards a few more came in and soon she had nine or ten. She was really happy to get the business.

The holiday season wasn't good for the restaurant business in those days.

Of course, sitting in a restaurant alone was never the best way to spend New Year's Eve. Brody could vouch for that, although he should have been used to being alone. In a way, maybe he was, if anyone ever gets used to it. He made it through Christmas that year by visiting his parents in Ottawa. Then he decided to stop in at the Bright Spot on the way back home. Why? he didn't know. Looking for something? Who knows? Then he heard Ellen talking about Charlie coming in and decided to wait for him. He had wanted to see Charlie for a long time, but couldn't work up the courage. He knew he needed to see him eventually, to tell him how he felt. He didn't expect him to understand. It was for him he needed to do it. If it helped him, that was great. A bonus. But he knew by then that he needed to do it for himself.

Then Ellen was talking directly to Ed. "Who were the four? Well I remember it like it was yesterday. There was Harry Jonas, Charlie Thomas, Andy Bingley and my Billy. That was when I met my Billy, you know. And Charlie was one of the originals. Hard to believe, now it's so many years later."

He could almost see them all sitting in the restaurant, although it did take some imagination, since the restaurant had been remodeled a few times since then. They had their food and midnight came when they were eating and they all shouted and sang and laughed and shook hands with each other. Then afterwards, they sat and talked until two in the morning, which was closing time. When they left, they all agreed to meet in the same place, at the same time the following year. They met every year since then, although of course their numbers diminished over the years. On the New Years' Eve Brody sat there and waited for Charlie, they were down to one.

"Never would o' thought that Charlie'd be the last one," said Ellen. "He was never the strongest one, you know. But he was lively. Why, he'd come bounding up those front steps three at a time and not even be breathing hard. And he'd talk the ear off the others. Couldn't get a word in edgewise with Charlie around. And that's saying something, eh?" She winked at me.

Brody forced a brief smile for her, and thought about Charlie Thomas. He could remember well the endless talking and teasing. Most of all, he remembered Sandy, his grand-daughter. He could almost see her light red hair and the freckles that covered her face and neck and shoulders. He could still feel the intensity with which she lived all the vivacity of her eighteen years. That was two years ago. How could two years seem so long and so short at the same time? Charlie lived in the apartment that had been added to her parent's house and whenever he went to visit, if she wasn't in the house, she was sure to be in the apartment. Brody's throat was starting to tighten as he tried to focus on Ellen.

She was saying that the gang started out with ten members. Over the years, they added a couple of men, but that was all. They called themselves the Pine Tree Gang because they had first met playing softball on the old field that used to be next to the high school. It was just a big field that was flat and grassy and a lot of kids played there. There was a great big pine tree at the far corner opposite to the high school but it was blown down in a big storm in 1940. There was just one year when they didn't meet. That was in 1941 when they were all overseas in the war.

After the war, they would all take a drink. It changed them to that extent. But they all became good upstanding citizens in the community. They were all professional men - lawyers, business men. And two of them were mayors and several were aldermen. They were smart, but they weren't just out to look after themselves. Eventually, they began to take on projects to help needy people around the community. There were lots of needy people around and some of the war veterans needed help too. They'd get someone to take money or food to people and once they paid a mortgage off for a guy who came home from the war with no legs. He died a few years ago and still had the same old house. Hardly anyone knew about it at the time, because that's the way the gang wanted it.

They used to sing a song at all their meetings. Their favourite was "It's a Long Way to Tipperary" and that became something of a theme song for them. After a few years of meetings, they always met in the back room of the restaurant. It was a cozy room and although it was sometimes used for small functions, everyone in town considered it the gang's room. There was a large stone fireplace and soft leather easy chairs and a big oak table they would gather around. Every time they came in, they'd sit and have their fish and chips and then Ellen would give them some fresh homemade pies and they'd drink a toast to each other. And they would talk and sing and laugh well into the night. Gradually, of course, they began to die off. There was always a wreath made from a pine branch placed on the casket. And they would sing their song at the funeral.

Brody saw Charlie Thomas at a funeral, but it wasn't for one of his gang. He didn't get to speak to him, because he was sitting with the other members of his family in the little room where the immediate family sits during funerals. The sight of that coffin would always be with him. It was fine light oak, with brass fittings and pots of flowers all around it. Inside were pink satin pillows and red ribbons and the profile of Sandy's freckled face and the light red hair, looking so beautiful and peaceful and so out of place.

They were out to a party with some friends in the country. They had too much beer to drink. Why did he insist on driving her home? Why did she go with him? Why did he take the lake road with all its bad curves? There are always lots of why's. Why's are the tortures of the damned. There are no answers. Or if there are, maybe we don't want to hear them. On the way home, the car left the road at Jason's corner by the lake and tumbled end over end down an eighty foot embankment into the water. The car landed upside down at the edge of the lake with its front end tilted down into the deeper water and she was hanging there upside down with her seat belt tight around her.

But the nightmare had only begun. The doors were jammed shut and the windows were closed and the water seeped slowly into the car. As the water level rose, she screamed for help and Brody frantically tried to release her seat belt, but it was stuck solid and she couldn't slide out of it. The water level rose in the car and he tried to keep her head above the surface until it became impossible. Afterwards, the water kept rising and he moved to the back of the car until his face was pressed against the cushions of the seat above his head and then in a last minute panic he managed to open a window and crawl out and find the surface. About that time, the police came and they called a tow truck and dragged the car out of the water. He left her there like that. There was nothing he could do. Some of the officers jumped into the water, but there was nothing they could do either.

He looked away from the window and wiped the tears from his eyes. They hadn't noticed, since Ellen was still telling her story. "When Andy died, they made a rule that they would meet each year and drink a toast to each other as long as there were two of them left to do it. They agreed that when there was just one left, the last survivor would drink a toast and break the glass on the fireplace and that would be that. So Charlie should be here about quarter to twelve." We sat and drank coffee and played the juke box and talked.

At exactly quarter to twelve, a small black Ford pulled up in front of the stairs and rolled to a stop. A young man jumped out and opened the back door and stood there. For what seemed like a long time, nothing happened. Then a white head slowly appeared. The young man reached down and put his arm gently around the old man, who slowly stood up and made his way to the stairs. Brody's heart started to pound as he recognized Charlie Thomas.

Holding tightly to the rail and the young man's arm, Charlie shuffled up the stairs one at a time. Ellen waited patiently at the door and when he was almost to the top, he saw her and a big smile stretched across his face. He moved a little faster and when he reached the top, she leapt forward and hugged him. Of course she was talking at the same time. "Charlie, Charlie, it's so good to see you. You're looking great. I'm so glad you could make it. Everything's ready."

As he entered the restaurant, he noticed Brody standing here and he stopped silently and stared. Ellen was suddenly silent, too. The only sound was coming from the juke box. Brody had rehearsed a thousand different lines, but now suddenly realized that he hadn't actually decided what he was going to say. He began to stammer. " Mr. Thomas, I want to tell you how sorry I am. How very sorry. Every day I've prayed for forgiveness. I - - -."

Charlie paused and then said, "I'm sorry too, kid, but there's nothing we can do to change anything. It's best to leave it alone." Then he turned and walked away with Ellen and I heard him saying, " How do you do it, young lady? You're even more beautiful than you were fifty years ago." Brody felt in a daze – still lurching forward with no place to go.

Charlie and Ellen talked their way all through the restaurant to the room at the back with Ed and Brody trailing silently behind them. Brody felt far away. They walked across the room and stood before the big oak table. Some logs were burning in the fireplace. A glass of brandy was standing on a linen place mat and Charlie's Victoria Cross lay beside it. On each of the other place mats around the table, there lay a Pine sprig. It was five to twelve. They all stood silently and then Ellen began to quietly sing the opening words of "It's a Long Way to Tipperary."

Charlie stood listening for a moment with his eyes fixed on the table. Then his back straightened up and he began to say the words with her. In and out of it. Missing lines and then picking them up again.

The mantle clock began to strike and they both stop singing and he picked up the glass and turned to face the fireplace. Then he raised the glass and said "So that's it, boys." And then as an afterthought, he said, "Welcome to Tipperary." He emptied the glass in one gulp and hurled it against the back of the fireplace where it shattered and fell to the hearth.

Then he turned and slowly left the room arm in arm with Ellen. As he passed Brodie, he leaned towards him and gently placed a hand on his shoulder and said "Come and sit with us, kid. I'll buy us a coffee." As they reached the swinging door, Ellen began talking again.

Brody sat down at the place where the brandy had been and brooded into the fire. The broken glass lay sparkling on the hearth. He wondered who would pick it up and what they would be thinking when they did. He supposed Ellen would clean up. It seemed most likely and maybe even appropriate. After a while, he noticed the animated sounds of chatter and laughter coming from the restaurant and stood and walked across the room and opened the door.

OF BEING AND TIME

When he woke up, Sarah was standing at the window facing the Atlantic, which stretched along a curved stony beach extending far away to the left and the right until it disappeared under the overgrown pine forests. Towards the open sea, there were several round, green islands among the cold, white-capped waves. Around Sarah's head were beams of sunlight that slanted in the window and danced with floating dust particles across the room.

"Today I am planning to go to town. A few matters have piled up, so I expect to be gone most of the day," he said.

She continued to face the window and said nothing.

He walked down the hall to the kitchen where he threw open the sliding doors to the patio and stood before the wide lawn sloping down to the beach. The air was fresh but cool and he closed the doors after a few moments.

"There's fall in the air today," he said, as he headed for the kettle to start the coffee.

As he sipped his coffee, he made a list on a small note pad of lined paper. The list contained five names, with several little items under each name. He sat and pondered the list, added an item and then pondered some more.

The telephone rang and he put the list down and walked into the kitchen to answer it. A voice came through impatiently "Dad, is that you? What were you doing?"

"Just getting my day moving," he replied. "What's up?

"I wondered if you were coming into town today."

"How much do you need, Billy?"

"It's not money," said his brother. "I have a great chance for a job but I need a drive to the interview. I thought if you were coming into town, maybe you wouldn't mind."

"Yeah, I'm coming in a little later and as long as it isn't too far, I'll take you there but I can't wait for you. See you in about an hour at the corner?"

"That'll be great. I can get a ride home."

After he hung up, he walked to his study and took some envelopes from his desk. Then he picked up the little pile of unpaid bills and started writing cheques for them. Soon all the bills were gone and he sealed the envelopes and put them in his jacket pocket. Then he went to the bedroom and tidied up the bed. Sarah was sitting in her favorite chair beside the window.

On the way out, he picked up his list and walked out-side and around the corner of the big white house to the car. Still being a driver at the age of eighty-six was something of which he was proud. They made him take a test when he turned eighty-five and he passed it with flying colors. He climbed behind the wheel of the old Buick and started it up.

As he drove down the winding lane to the coast road, he looked back up to the wide bedroom window and waved. She was waving back and smiling. Then he drove past the small fenced-in graveyard on the broad expanse of lawn where two gravestones stood facing the ocean. He turned left on the road and accelerated.

Billy was waiting at the first corner as he entered the town.

"Hi, Dad."

"And how are you this morning, young man?" Billy had turned forty-five a few days ago.

"Good. I think this is it. My big break. I met this guy last night and he's opening up a restaurant - a nice fancy one. They'll serve drinks and everything. He needs a waiter. And he says I might be able to cook, too. I always wanted to be a chef. Just like those fancy French guys."

"Well, you worked bussing tables one summer, so you have some experience."

"That's what I told him," said Billy.

John looked out the side window at a dog squatting on a lawn.

"What time is your appointment?"

"Eight o'clock."

"It's eight-thirty now."

"Yeah, but he's a good shit. He won't mind."

They drove the ten blocks to the old fire station by the tracks. A big sign hung over the wide doors. JAKE'S DINER OPENING JULY 15. TWO BEERS FOR THE PRICE OF ONE.

Before Billy got out, John reached over and placed his hand on his shoulder. "Listen, kid, take care. And call Langford in the morning."

"Why, is he sick?"

"No, but I want you to call him, OK?"

"OK, bro, see you later."

As he drove away, Billy stood with a puzzled expression and watched him go.

The bank didn't open until ten and he had a appointment with Marshall, his lawyer, at eleven, so there was still some time. He went first to the telephone company, and asked to pay his bill.

The young woman smiled up at his six-foot-four frame topped off with thick white hair and asked "Do you have the bill with you, sir?"

"No, I didn't get it yet. It should be coming any time, but I thought you would have a record of the amount."

"Excuse me, you want to pay your bill before receiving it?" She laughed. "I've heard of keeping a good credit rating, but - - -" He laughed with her.

"That's important, you know. When I was a young fellow, we didn't have debts. Not unless we were in trouble. I thought you might have the amount on your computer. Here's an old statement with the account number on it."

She clicked on her keyboard for a few moments and then said "You owe twenty dollars and thirty-one cents. The bill was sent out yesterday, so you should get it today or tomorrow. Sure you don't want to wait for it?"

"No. I'll pay it now." And he gave her the money, took his receipt and stuffed it in his pocket.

He drove back down to Main Street and pulled into the parking lot behind the bank. Before long, the bank opened and he went inside and closed his two savings accounts and transferred the money into a single account, the joint one he kept with Langford. Then he went to his safety deposit box and stuffed some papers into his jacket. After a brief chat with his old friend, the manager, he went out and walked up the street to Marshall's office.

Marshall was leaning back in his chair with his feet on the desk reading a brochure about Scotland. When John came in, he started talking without looking up.

"Mornin', John. Planning a little golf trip. You should come."

"I'm too old for that anymore."

"Oh, go on, if I had half your energy, I'd be president of the bank by now. You've got years left in you."

John's eyes twinkled. "Time catches us all, Marshall, and then we can feel the reaper's hot breath on our neck. They say that when your time comes and you look quickly over your left shoulder, you might sometimes catch a glimpse of him."

Marshall laughed. "You're very morose this morning, John."

John laughed, too. "It's a beautiful morning. I came to make some changes in my will."

"Of course, what would you like to do?"

"I want to appoint Langford as the executor and I'd like to leave all the property to him."

"All of it?"

"Yes. Billy would only let it run to ruin or sell it and waste the money. I want enough money to stay in capital to provide him a lifetime allowance of five hundred dollars a month. That should make up for the property."

"Would you like to wait while we make up the papers? It'll only take a few minutes."

"Yes. I'd like that. Thank you."

When he walked out into the fresh outside air, John took a deep breath and then walked the three blocks to the Bistro. Langford was sitting at a table by the sidewalk watching for him.

"You're early", said John as he pulled out a chair and sat down.

"I thought I heard some urgency in your voice, so I couldn't work."

"Sorry, I didn't mean to sound that way. I just had a lot to do today, I guess."

"I know I haven't been around the past few days. The lawn must need mowing."

"It's not bad. Been dry lately. Anyway, I can do it."

"I worry about you doing it. How about I drop around in the morning and give a hand?"

"Actually, I was going to suggest that you drop around. There's no hurry about the lawn, though. There's another job for you."

"What's up?"

"You'll know when you get there."

"Why so mysterious?"

Langford was looking concerned but also relaxed and serious. He had that thoughtful air he always carried and looked every inch the retired professor he was. His question hung there unanswered.

"How's the book going", asked John. "You seem to be busier since you retired."

"It's only early retirement. I wanted to do some research and lucked into some research funds. The book is going great. I decided to place more emphasis on Sartre than on Heideigger. I've always felt that Sartre was the greatest modern existentialist and people can relate more clearly to his war experiences and their impact on his theories. Heideigger is more obscure, to most people anyway."

"It's all kind of obscure to me, although I enjoyed reading Sartre years ago, especially his novels."

Their lunch lasted late into the afternoon. Then they walked back to his car together and they hugged before he unlocked the door and got in. Langford promised to be at the house by eight o'clock in the morning.

Later, driving up the lane, John passed the headstones facing the sea, one for a single grave and the other a double with two ovals on its face. One of the ovals had a name inscribed in it and the other one was blank. He paused but not for long. He was anxious to be home.

Sarah was standing in the window watching for him as he knew she would be. He waved and she waved back with a big smile. He hurried as fast as he could up the stairs and opened the door. He would skip supper tonight. He would go to bed early. She would be waiting.

THE SAVIOR

It was a pleasant day on the Gulf coast, but cooler than usual for November. Rob and Sally sat at a picnic table by the Coastal road to Mexico, feeling the hot Texas sun on their shoulders as it peeked through the gaps in the clouds. They were eating burritos they had bought at a roadside stand a few miles back and washing them down with bottled water.

Out in the center of the gulf, a late season hurricane was passing by, and the waves had been whipped up higher than usual. Sometimes they crashed on the rocks far below with a loud roar and sprayed high in the air. The young couple were lost in their thoughts.

Rob heard the crunching noise of tires on gravel and, looking down by the road, saw an old black Lincoln pulling up behind their car, which was parked on the shoulder. He judged the Lincoln to be about ten years old. It was rusted and dirty, with dents and scratches all over it. It had tinted windows, but inside Rob could make out the dark outlines of three men.

As the car rolled to a stop in a cloud of dust, the driver got out and looked up towards them with a wide toothy smile. He wore a rumpled black suit, black riding boots with tin buckles on them and a small sombrero. Even from the distance, Rob could see that the suit was a cheap shiny material and was way too small.

The man was fat and large, probably about two hundred eighty pounds. He tipped his sombrero, still smiling, and Rob caught a glimpse of black spiky hair that looked like it hadn't been washed for a month. The stranger started up the twenty-odd stairs between the picnic table and the cars.

As he laboured up the stairs, the big man broke out into a copious sweat and stopped a couple of times to wipe his brow and catch his breath. This, despite the fact it was getting colder. A chill wind started up from the ocean and a dark cloud covered the sun, making the day suddenly dark and gloomy. It looked like rain.

Sally shivered and Rob touched her hand as they watched the man climbing the stairs. Fighting a rising feeling of apprehension, Rob looked around but there was no place to go, with the water below them on one side, the stairs on the other and the mesquite brush and rocks all around.

As the labouring blob of a man came closer, still smiling, Rob could see the gaps in his teeth, and the several-day old beard stubble. Their burritos forgotten, the two young people watched their visitor arrive at the top of the stairs. As he did so, he stumbled slightly on the top stair. When he leaned forward to catch himself, Rob saw a revolver inside the man's coat, under his arm.

They could smell his breath now, reeking of stale tortil-las and tequila. Now that he was close enough, they could see the pocked and scarred face. One eye had been dam-aged and looked up towards the brim of the sombrero. The other gleamed at them with a cold, absent stare. Both Sally and Rob were shivering.

"Buenos Dias, muchacho", he said in a rough, husky and breathless voice "Que passa?".

"Buenos Dias, Senor", mumbled Rob.

The big man switched to English "Do you know the way to Corpus Christi?"

Rob tried to keep his voice under control, knowing that he was no match for this creature with the gun, knowing they were at his mercy. Rob glanced back down the road behind him and said "That way. About two hundred miles." When his eyes returned to the stranger, he was looking down the barrel of the revolver. He stared transfixed at the huge cannon-like opening.

"Dinero, muchacho. Your money. All of it. And fast."

Sally issued a muffled scream.

The big man stepped towards her and Rob instinctively moved in front of him.

The hand with the gun swiped hard, grazing Rob on the head and knocking him down. Rob sat there on the ground, looking up. Frozen still. And stunned.

Sally stepped backwards involuntarily, the visitor leaned forward, leering into her face and grabbed her shirt, ripping it and revealing her bra. She screamed again and he laughed "Very pretty." She clutched the golden crucifix hanging on her chest, hoping that was what the man meant.

The sound of a car door came from below. Sally glanced down and saw a skinny man heading up the stairs. She saw to her horror that he was carrying a big machete. Something shiny swung from his neck over his shirt as he stumbled up the stairs. He had on dirty jeans – the filthiest she could ever have imagined, and a white tee shirt turned dark yellow grey from sweat and dirt. On his face was a grin, absolutely humourless. As he drew nearer, she saw that his eyes were very dark, such that the whites stood out almost in a glow. She began to shake uncontrollably. Rob sat on the ground and gasped for air.

A break in the cloud cover allowed a shaft of sunlight through, which glanced across the road and moved up the hill with the new stranger. As he drew closer, she could make out the sores on his face and neck. She saw the shiny thing swinging on his neck was a tinny medallion – one that he could have found in a tourist store, or on a tourist - imprinted with the Madonna, which clinked on his metal buttons as he climbed the stairs.

Sally screamed desperately, "Oh God, help us!"

The big man swiped her with the back of his hand, opening a cut in her lip. Just as the skinny stranger reached the top, some drops of her blood fell from her lip and onto her crucifix, running down the body of Christ, which at that moment, was illuminated by the ray of sunlight which had made its way up the hill. Seeing this, the skinny man stopped still and crossed himself. "Santa Maria", he shouted and waved the machete at the big man. "We must go," he said. Pulling the big man down the stairs and looking back fearfully, he said "We must go quickly."

THE WIND HARP

She came to him on a salty night in late fall when the leaves graced the ground and the moon was teasing the dark.

He slouched in his easy chair in the parlour, a log burning in the fireplace, and a half finished drink in his hand. The night was chilly, but it was warm and cozy inside.

"This is not so bad," said the brandy.

"It could be worse," he agreed vaguely.

The doorbell rang.

"Damn," he said as he struggled to his feet, "I thought that would be all for tonight."

Back to the vestibule, picking up a couple of candy baskets along the way, opening the door and looking down for a little gremlin or ghost, seeing high black boots, and then scanning up a slim, dark frame, past curved thighs covered in a long black skirt, up to a black wool sweater rounded out by nicely proportionate breasts to a very beautiful face, framed with jet black hair and topped with a black tam.

She extracted a candy from one of the baskets with a smile. "Thank you, Sir. Uh, trick or treat?"

He fumbled through a reply. "Of course, have another one. Indeed, do."

She produced a copy of the day's newspaper, waving the classifieds, and then he understood and stepped back for her as she entered.

"You wish to hire a housekeeper, I believe," she said.

"Yes," he replied. "My wife died a year ago, and my last housekeeper just moved away for a better job."

He clicked the door shut. He hadn't expected anyone to drop in. Others had called and made an appointment in a public place. A man living alone advertising for a female housekeeper might present certain perils, might call for searching questions.

She flowed to the parlour and posed in the chair opposite his. He had to rush, after showing her the way. He had once seen a cheetah run down a deer on a dusty plain. The deer had seemed slow and awkward by comparison.

But she didn't seem very dangerous. Her green eyes glowed with courteous expectation and sparkled in the firelight. She looked through him and he shivered. He offered her a drink, which she declined and he sipped the Brandy.

She was new in town and had no references, but she had experience looking after her ailing mother and sister –

before they died, the last of her family. Her other experience was in music. She asked if he would mind her practicing and he said it would be fine, because her room would be in the extra wing and quite separate from the main part of the house.

He had many questions and she answered them unhesitatingly and clearly. She was self assured and well spoken.

"I studied in Paris," she said. After leaving home in the northern countryside of Wales. We were quite well off, so I had a wide range of choice. My love is the harp, I do a good job of the work I do, but I do it so I can play. When I can earn my living from playing, that is all I do."

She spoke matter-of-factly.

He agreed to hire her and arranged to meet her the next day so she could move in her possessions.

The house became more spotless than he could ever remember, even before in what seemed a previous life when he was not alone. And she seemed to keep a quiet lifestyle, working regularly and in the evenings playing her harp. He soon began leaving the door open to listen to her, listening to the strange lyrical melodies which he had never heard before. They were songs of the ancient Celts. Songs going back to the earliest years of Britain.

"I love your music," he whispered from the doorway. "I now know why harps are so often associated with angels.

159

Golden harps." He whispered because he did not want to destroy the mood of her music.

She laughed. A light joyful sound to his jaded ears. A sound he suddenly realized he hadn't heard for a long time. "It's a very old paint. Not gold, I'm afraid. But in certain light - - " She shrugged. "Perhaps."

And it was indeed a unique harp. It had white strings, and golden knobs where they joined the curves of the wood. The base was of black mahogany polished to a high sheen. But it was the sound that stood out - clear and pure like the air of the mountains in the morning, like the water that babbles and splashes its way down rocky slopes.

"It was passed down for many generations in my family," said Elinor. "Nobody knows how many. It is my job to pass it along to one who will love it as much as I."

After a few months, during the summer, she moved the harp to the back porch. There, she played it in the evenings and sometimes he played along with her with his classical guitar. It had been his only friend for over a year. She began to teach him some of the Celtic tunes, and then one night late in the summer, they made love in the sitting room, with the door open to the evening breeze. While they were together, he was startled because he heard the harp begin to play.

"It is the wind from the mountains," she said. "It you leave it there and if all is right, the strings will move of their own accord – they will play the music of the wind."

Later he heard her playing at a folk festival in a field near the sea. She sat in a small tent that flapped heavily in the breeze coming in with the tide. He wandered in part way through her performance and stretched on the ground near a tent-pole in the middle of the sparse audience.

She was sitting on a wooden stage in a long, blue cotton dress and leather sandals. Her hair hung forward over her shoulders as she leaned in to pluck the strings. She closed her eyes and swayed very slightly with the melodies. Occasionally, her eyes swept over the people sitting on the grass and out towards the rolling sea in the distance. Sometimes her eyes smiled a little when they met his.

He felt strangely peaceful as he walked with her across the field to the row of tents at the edge of the soccer field, carrying the harp to her van. He went back every day to see her as long as the festival lasted.

That fall, exactly one year to the day, she left in the night. She took nothing with her. Absolutely nothing. Someone thought they saw her walking by the sea. A couple out for a late stroll thought they passed her standing in a field. People looked for a few days, but found nothing. There was no one he knew to contact. She had always been vague about where she had come from.

The moon danced in the breeze. The grass waved. Two deer appeared across the river from dank woods and he stiffened. Watching like the trees. Breathing like the earth. They muzzled the water, eyes darting. Ever alert. Then they jumped and were gone. Were they ever there? Were they real? He stood up and walked back up the trail to the house, carefully because the skunks might be up and about.

The bushes had gone black. Like the bears that had been following the river. A mother and her cub. Living off the river and its inhabitants. Moving leisurely always, sometimes in the interval and sometimes upstream in the higher ground.

The ancient harp stands alone on the back porch. It is late evening. In the background to the north, the rugged mountains loom dark against the sky. A wind flows in from the mountains and across the clipped fields, bringing a cool dampness and the smell of fresh-cut hay.

He sits back in his favourite easy chair with his eyes closed. He is in the sitting room, just inside the sliding screen door to the porch. He breathes deeply of the mountain breezes and listens carefully to the sounds of the harp. After a time, he hears the tune of Ton Alarch. "She brought me joy and she brought me sorrow," he says to himself. "But she left me peace."

Ton Alarch is one of his favourites, and the one that Elinor most likes to play. No doubt it is her Welsh heritage. Her Celtic leanings.